BAXTER

LAST MAN STANDING

KATHLEEN LAWLESS

Cover design by M. Macphail

ISBN print: 978-1-989873-42-7

To my three wonderful, supportive children and all their expressions of creativity.

PROLOGUE

Baxter Reid tapped his beer glass with a spoon to get everyone's attention. It took awhile, a series of ssshhh's running through the room full of guys, most of whom had a drink or two under their belts. He knew them all, had worked with most of them and somehow over the years, wound up as the unofficial spokesperson at every industry stag.

He cleared his throat. "We're gathered here to give our buddy Blaze a suitable sendoff on his foray into the land of matrimony." He paused and took a sip. "I gotta tell you, I'm as surprised by this development as the rest of you. Blaze and I were the last of the Mohicans, the last two amigos here at the studio to decree we'd never dip our toes into the troubled waters," jeers and boos greeted his words the way he intended, "pardon me, the warm and welcoming waters of married life. Which leaves me the last man standing, the last bachelor in captivity, a title I fully intend to defend till I draw my last breath.

"Blaze, thanks for making me the reigning champ of avoiding the mat trap. And seriously, buddy, all the best. For those of you who don't know, Blaze is getting married in a couple of weeks, two entire states north in the beautiful Pacific Northwest, on some tiny bump in the ocean called Blue Sky Island. After sampling and rejecting more than his share of single women in California, our friend met his match in Washington State, the sister of an old friend, no less. All of which tells me to avoid west coast islands and any old friends who might have an unmarried sister. Amen!"

"What about the married sisters?" someone yelled.

The room rocked with laughter. Baxter waited for the guests to settle down, then raised his glass. "To Blaze."

The others echoed his toast as he locked gazes across the room with his old friend. Kidding aside, he was happy for Blaze, who after cinching his title as the World's Greatest Stuntman, was now stepping back to help choreograph stunts in Baxter's next film and train Hollywood's new generation of stunt doubles.

Baxter looked around the room with a wry smile. Right now, there was no one single to take Blaze's place as wingman when he went out on the town. A few years from now, half these guys would likely be divorced.

He spotted Mike, his agent, across the room and made his way there slowly. He listened to the chatter for a few minutes before he caught Mike's eye and the agent joined him on the circle's outskirts.

"Don't even ask," Mike said.

"What?" Baxter widened his eyes in an expression of mock-innocence.

"I know you, buddy. I also know you're hurting for the *Sentry* shoot."

"You know I'd be a natural to direct it."

"Nothing's been decided yet. MCU is taking their time with the rights."

"Did I hear rumors Hurst's interested?"

"You and the entire free world," Mike said.

"So what's the deal?"

"The deal is, so far, there is no deal."

Baxter narrowed his gaze. Could Mike know more than he was saying? "I'm counting on you to keep me updated."

"If the deal gets struck, I'll make sure you're on the list."

Not good enough!

"Anyone can get on the list. How do I get to the top of the list?"

Mike rocked back on his heels. "Ever read what's written about you?"

"Why would I?"

"Well, the studios do. The production houses do. The backers do."

"What? Are you saying I'm a bad risk? Show me a more bankable director in the industry. You know what my last film grossed on opening week?"

"Of course I do."

"Right." Baxter switched tactics. No point antagonizing someone who professed to be in his camp.

"All I'm saying is that you have less than a boy scout image."

"Show me a boy scout who can come close to me in the director's chair."

"Hey, Bax. It's all about the public's perception. Anyway, enough shop talk. Tonight is all about Blaze."

As Baxter watched Mike walk away, he couldn't ignore the niggling feeling the agent was up to something.

CHAPTER 1

April Thomas stopped at the studio security gate and gave the guard her name to check against the list of approved visitors. Moments later he passed her a visitor badge, the barricade rose, and she drove through to the parking lot where she found an empty spot and raised the roof on her Audi convertible. LA's sunny September weather meant the leather seats in her car would be sizzling if she left the roof down.

Earlier, she'd googled Sound Stage D's location, along with everything she could learn on-line about Baxter Reid. The guy kept a fairly low social media profile, which didn't stop others from gleefully taking his name in vain.

A perfectionist, he apparently had a healthy ego and a growing anti-fan club of disgruntled actors, grips, stage-hands and stunt doubles. All of which could be taken as a container load of sour grapes, but there were a few red flags she needed to turn forest green. Like a lot of the people April had worked with in the past, Baxter Reid was his own worst enemy.

He never smiled and made nice for the press. He

expected everyone else to hold themselves to his exacting standards. And it appeared he had no patience for political correctness, equal opportunity, or diversity of any kind.

Family background was skimpy. A military brat, oldest of two boys, the family had moved a lot, mostly overseas. Father deceased, no mention of the mother. Today, she was about to meet the twice-nominated-for-an-academy-award director face to face.

"There you are, April." Baxter's agent, Mike Cameron had obviously been watching for her and hurried to her side the second she set foot inside the sound stage. "Right on time."

Mike was typical Hollywood. Fake tan, fake veneers, and muscles courtesy of a gym rather than hard work. He had an impressive client roster, most of whom didn't need her services so she had not met him in person until today.

She looked around at what appeared to be organized chaos as people in headsets clutching clipboards ran back and forth. Here and there several other groups stood in small huddles. "Where's Baxter Reid?"

Mike flashed her a dazzling look at his veneers. "He's uh, he's tied up for a little bit."

April narrowed her gaze. "But he *is* expecting me."

Mike didn't look the slightest bit uneasy. "Not exactly. Bax is a seat of his pants kind of guy, and I find the element of surprise is best where he's concerned. Too much notice of upcoming change gives him far too much time to find fault with whatever's headed his way."

"Don't directors need to be organized and focused?"

"Well, sure. They also need to be able to weather anything unexpected."

"Hmmph." April crossed her arms over her chest. "You mean like someone hired to improve his social standing?"

More blinding dazzle from the veneers. Just then, the decibel level dropped as Holly Snow, media darling and star of the movie currently being filmed appeared with Baxter on her heels.

"She looks smaller in person," April said. She'd lived in LA long enough to not be starstruck every time she saw a celebrity and had worked with more than a few. No matter how famous, stars were just people, more often than not hiding behind a fancy façade to disguise their insecurities.

"I don't know his secret, but Baxter manages to make her look bigger on screen. Otherwise, viewers would know her stunt double does all the real work."

Her eyes followed Holly Snow. "Is it true Baxter Reid never hires female stunt people?"

"They call them stuntmen for a reason."

April spun around. How had he managed that? Snuck up behind them without being seen.

"I didn't know you'd be dropping by today, Mike." His words might be directed to his agent but his eyes were taking her measure. 'Not pretty enough to be an actress', shifted to 'What are you doing here with Mike?'

"Baxter Reid, April Thomas," Mike said breezily. "I didn't know I needed an appointment."

"*You* don't. But you know I don't appreciate strangers on the set."

"Hopefully you two won't be strangers for long," Mike said.

"Latest Tinder date?" Baxter asked sarcastically.

"Revitalique," Mike said, not very helpfully.

Baxter's brow furrowed. "Is that a new dating ap?"

"Not," April said, tired of being talked about as if she wasn't there. "It's an agency specializing in image makeovers."

"Good," Baxter said. "Mike could use one." He turned as if to leave them.

"I'm not here for Mike," April said.

Baxter did a half turn, waiting. She could almost see the numbers clicking through his brain, two plus two equaling four.

April met his gaze straight on. "I'm here for you."

BAXTER FINISHED his turnabout in slow motion and gave Mike a dirty look. "Your idea?"

"Just doing my job to secure you the deal of your dreams."

Baxter crossed his arms over his chest and waved away his first AD who was bearing down on them. "Tell everybody to take ten," he snapped. Then he turned back to his uninvited guests, starting with the woman. Medium length straight dark hair, average size and stature, Botox-free, judging by the expressive way she raised her brow. On first glance nothing exceptional about her, except—something he wasn't able to quite put his finger on. And something he had the sudden urge to figure out.

He turned his attention to Mike. "What makes you think I can't get the *Sentry* gig based on my track record?"

"It's not your film-making track record," Mike said. "I had a tip recently from someone on the inside that they're less than impressed with your social standing."

"Social standing?" Baxter scoffed. "You and I both know the only thing those guys care about is opening week profits."

"It's not that simple anymore. If the general public decides someone is persona non grata, their career is pretty much in the toilet, no matter their earlier favor or body of work."

"So a bunch of idiots glued to their phones get to decide the fate of the industry?"

"That's a bit simplistic, but—"

"But not far off the mark," April said. "Public perception goes a long way. Yours leaves a lot to be desired."

All he heard was the way she wrapped her tongue around the word *desired*. He hadn't imagined her voice. It was like a cool breeze on a hot day, inviting, enticing, addictive. And in some extraordinary way, matched her look. You just knew there was something out of the ordinary about her.

"I've never given a crap about the public's perception of me."

"That much is obvious."

He didn't like the way this conversation was going. "I've got to get to work. Paying these guys overtime murders the budget."

Mike just nodded and smiled. "I just wanted you two to meet. April's known for her magic touch when it comes to improved social standing."

He gave her a lazy look, disappointed when it didn't have the desired effect; to send her cowering. "Is that a fact?"

She handed him her card. "Tonight. Eight o'clock. I'll text you the location. We'll formulate a plan."

"We're shooting late tonight."

She shook her head. "Actually, you're not. Your star has a special appearance booked at six, and the production is scheduled to wrap by five at the latest."

Baxter blew out a breath and turned on his heel, calling over his shoulder. "Then get off the set and let me get to work."

Behind him, he heard Mike say to April, "That went well."

He didn't catch her response.

BAXTER WAS SORELY TEMPTED to do a no-show. Sadly, he knew it would solve nothing. Once Mike had a target in his sights he never let up. Precisely what made him such a successful agent. Mike knew how badly Baxter wanted a shot at *Sentry*, assuming the powers-that-be ironed out the details and the project was a go. Live action rights to comic book characters could be tricky.

He arrived at the address that had shown up this afternoon in his text messages. He'd been expecting a bar or restaurant, but Google Maps had taken him to a residential street in Jefferson Park. He parked at the curb and waited. The address was an unlit coffee shop with a closed sign on the door, which deepened the puzzle. April Thomas didn't strike him as the type to send someone on a wild goose chase.

He got out of his car, pulled out his phone and rechecked the address. He was just about to shoot off a text when a sleek black town car pulled up. The backdoor closest to him opened and the interior light flashed on, revealing April Thomas inside, her skirt riding up high enough to display an intriguing length of leg.

"You're right on time."

He'd been thinking about her voice all afternoon, trying to capture what made it so captivating and had almost convinced himself he was imagining things. But nope! Her words poured over him like warm rain, awakening his senses.

"Actually, I was early." He preferred scoping a place out in advance. He wasn't a fan of surprises, and Mike knew it. When she showed no signs of alighting, he got in and closed the door behind him. "Fancy meeting you here."

As the car accelerated away from the curb, she pushed a button and a panel opened to reveal a built-in bar. "Drink?"

"Whatever you're having."

As he'd guessed, a glass of overpriced mineral water with a wedge of lime found its way into his hand.

She sat back with her drink, not saying a word.

He looked into his glass, then up at her. "I take it you like being in control of a situation."

"I find a mobile office suits my needs more than bricks and mortar. Shall we get started?"

"In a minute," Baxter said, feeling the need to at least put his hand on the reins. "Even if you don't have an office, why here instead of a bar or restaurant?"

"LA is a very public town. I find this affords more privacy."

"Ah. So the general public has no idea I'm about to become your latest project, which they might have reason to speculate about if we were seen together."

A cool smile greeted him. "Are you? About to become my latest project?"

"I am according to Mike. I don't see the need, personally."

"You're not exactly the darling of the press these days."

He leaned closer. "Afraid you'll be tainted by association?"

"My job is to not only make over your image, but to have the changes appear to be organic."

"Like I suddenly saw the light?"

"Or turned into a human being with depth of character."

"Ouch. Are you saying I come across as shallow?"

"You don't come across at all."

He rapped on the partition between them and the driver. "I think I've heard everything I need to hear." The driver kept going.

She held his gaze. "Do you trust Mike?"

"Up until now, I did. Now I'm wondering just what he's got me into."

She took his untouched mineral water from his hand and mixed him a Negroni. "I understand this is more to your taste." He took a tentative sip. The woman knew her cocktails.

"What else did you learn about me?"

"Nothing I'd put much store by. You eschew social media. You're a serial dater, judging by all the posts from disenchanted dates, very few of whom made it as far as girl-friend status."

"Is that a black mark?"

"It would certainly be a red flag if I was looking for a relationship, but some women can't resist a challenge."

He leaned forward. "Including you?"

She refused the bait. "You have a very clear career goal. One I can help you achieve. If you cooperate. The catch is, any change has to look genuine."

"What can I tell you? I'm a genuine kind of guy."

She raised one brow in a way that implied she didn't believe it for a second. "Good. Because here's what I have in mind.

CHAPTER 2

Baxter hadn't exactly waxed enthusiasm when she outlined a few ideas on how best to improve his social standing, but he hadn't been totally resistant the way he had at the studio earlier. Maybe he'd had some time to think about it and accept that she and Mike had his best interests at heart.

She was fine-tuning her initial thoughts as she looked over the schedule for Baxter that Mike had provided, when her doorbell rang, startling her. Very few people knew where she lived and those who did knew better than to bother her on a work day. It could be the courier, although she'd not been texted to expect a delivery. She picked up her phone and checked her security camera. Her half-sister Mackenzie stood on the porch with three-year-old Liam in her arms.

"Oh, thank goodness you're here." Mackenzie pushed past her to the living room and unloaded Liam and his backpack into a chair near the TV.

"It's a work day," April said mildly.

"I know and I'm sorry, but I'm desperate. I just got a call-back from a recent audition. I tried everyone I could think of, but no luck." She turned and made a praying motion with her hands. "Pretty please. I'll only be an hour. He has a movie to watch." She smoothed back a lock of red-gold hair from Liam's forehead. "You'll be a good boy for Aunty April, won't you?"

Liam gave her an angelic smile and head nod that reminded April so much of their father, then dug into his backpack for a plastic container of cheerios and a tablet. In seconds a movie appeared on the screen and he was watching with rapt attention. Were kids born knowing how to do that these days?

April started to tell him he couldn't eat in here, then stopped. What was a few crumbs?

Mackenzie swooped in, dropped a kiss on the top of his head and turned toward April. "Thanks, Sis. I owe you." Then she was gone.

"Aunty will be in her office, Liam."

Liam nodded without looking up. April paused at the doorway and looked back at her little charge. Hadn't she read someplace that too much screentime wasn't good for developing minds?

She returned to her office, happy to see an email from the volunteer coordinator at the Children's Hospital wanting to know when Antman and the show's director were available. Baxter had begrudgingly given her the contact information for Antman's agent, her next email.

Men were funny creatures. He'd balked at the hospital visit idea until she suggested he take a popular superhero in costume with him. The kids would be more excited to meet Antman but Baxter, as the film's director, would have a chance to present a behind-the-camera side.

"Aunty April?"

Shoot, she'd forgotten about Liam. He stood in the doorway to her office looking adorable in his Oshkosh overalls and denim jacket. An outfit she'd gotten him for his last birthday after Mackenzie's not-so-subtle hints. "What is it, sweetie?"

"I'm thirsty."

"Did mommy send a sippy cup?"

"I drank it all. And I went pee."

Hopefully in the bathroom. She thought quickly. No juice or milk in the fridge. "Do you want a glass of water?"

He shook his head emphatically in a way she knew mineral water would receive a similar reaction. She glanced at her watch. Mackenzie had said an hour, but April knew that had been an optimistic estimate.

"Shall we walk down to the store and see what they have?" She didn't know much about kids, but she knew a special seat was required to transport one around by car.

"Okay," Liam said with a heavy sigh that made him sound far older than his years. Suddenly she was struck by what his life must be like. Mackenzie, a single mom, had moved in with her parents while she tried to get her acting career back on track after she had Liam. April suspected he got shuffled around a lot between friends and family, everyone trying to help Mackenzie get back on her feet. The identity of Liam's father was a well-kept secret and whoever it was, he'd never been in the picture. She wondered if he even knew he had a son. Maybe it was better for everyone that he didn't.

"Don't you go to school?"

He shook his head.

April wondered why not as she grabbed her phone, purse and keys. He was bright enough and would benefit from interacting with other kids his own age. "Next year?"

He just shrugged his tiny shoulders.

Out on the sidewalk, she took his hand firmly in hers. It was baby soft and pudgy and she pressed an impulsive kiss to his dimpled knuckles.

"How's Popa and Mel? I mean Nana," she said quickly when his brow furrowed. Her father had married Mel when April was five. Mackenzie had been born a year later, making Mackenzie Mel's third daughter. They must have wanted a boy real bad because they kept going and produced two sons. Two steps and three half-siblings for April on that side of the family. Their house had always been bedlam. For Liam's sake, she hoped it was calmer these days. She did her best to duck invitations to birthday parties and holidays like Easter and Thanksgiving or Christmas. Sadly, she did the same thing with her mother's extended family as well.

"Okay, I guess. Popa sleeps a lot."

April rolled her eyes. Some things never changed. She didn't remember a time when her father wasn't sprawled out in his lazy boy chair after a meal, snoring loudly while the TV droned on in the background.

At the store she bought Liam a smoothie, telling herself it was a healthy treat made from fruit and other good stuff. On the way back to the house he stopped and stared longingly across the street at the small playground in the one corner of the park.

"Would you like to go play for a few minutes? Not long because your mom will be back soon." His delighted smile was the only answer she needed.

"We'll cross down there, at the crosswalk," she said. Never too soon to teach children some road sense and traffic safety.

They reached the playground and Liam left her with his

drink as he raced over to the monkey bars. April watched him clamber to the top, her heart in her throat. Should he be going that high? She looked around and saw a young woman, probably a nanny, riding herd on a couple of children racing around and teasing each other.

"Liam," she called, edging closer. Not that it would do any good. If he fell, she'd hardly be in a position to catch him.

"Most kids know their own limits," said a woman standing nearby.

"Really?"

"First time here?" asked the woman, companionably. "You've got that frantic deer-in-the-headlights look."

"Is it that obvious?"

"Lillian Swagle." The woman's hand came April's way as she introduced herself.

"April Thomas, terrified and inexperienced aunt and babysitter," she admitted.

"April Thomas," the woman mused. "Why do I know that name?"

"I don't know, but I'm pretty sure I'd remember you if we'd met." Lillian was nearly six feet tall with thick, curling, waist-length brown hair, not someone she'd forget meeting.

"We haven't met," Lillian said. "But I know the name." She stared off into the distance. "Not PR but close. Social media influencer?"

"Not exactly," April said.

"Revitalize. Reputation. Image. Am I warm?"

"Very warm," April said, taken aback. She'd helped a vast roster of clients, but kept as low a profile as possible.

Lillian nodded as if pleased. "I knew it. I'm on the board of the Global Fund for Women. Your name was recently bandied about. We'll be electing a new board soon."

"I've heard of your group," April said. "You do good work."

"We haven't even scratched the surface," Lillian said. "Whenever I get frustrated, I remind myself about the suffragettes and the challenges they faced. It helps put things in perspective." She pulled a card from the back pocket of her jeans. "Drop me an email when you get the chance. We're working on something substantial and it would be good to get your input."

"I'm flattered but I'm not sure I have time to take on—"

"Not even to come out to support our annual fundraising dinner and auction?"

April turned the card over in her hand. "Now that you mention it—aren't your fundraising dinners invitation only?"

Lillian's dark eyes were dancing with humor. "We've discovered the more exclusive the event, the more we can charge and the better caliber of guests and press coverage."

"Smart," April said. "I recall hearing that if you only attend one event a year, this is the one."

"How kind of you to say so. I'll see you're at my table. Will you be bringing a plus-one?"

"No, I—Yes. Yes, I will. I know just the right person."

Lillian raised a brow. "I bet you do."

Just then April's phone beeped. She pulled it out and peered at the screen which was hard to read in the sunlight. "My sister's back finally. Come on, Liam," she called. "Mom's waiting." She turned to Lillian. "It was great to meet you. I'll drop you an email as soon as I get home."

"If you don't, know that I'll stalk you," Lillian said. "I'm really glad we ran into each other."

"Me too."

THE BELL RANG. Baxter and his opponent approached each other and did the boxer's version of a high five, gloved right hands overhead lightly bouncing off each other. Baxter climbed through the boxing ring ropes, spat out his mouth guard and started to unlace one glove with his teeth. Kelvin did the same. Gloves off, Baxter flexed his fingers.

"Who was I today?" Kelvin asked mildly, as he swiped his forearm across his forehead. Baxter picked up his discarded towel, wiped his face and slung the towel around his neck.

"No one," Baxter said shortly. Maybe Mike. It wouldn't be seemly to take a swing at a lady, even if April Thomas did arouse those kinds of instincts.

"Hey, man, I know the only reason you're here is to work out your frustrations. Usually human-caused."

Baxter barked out a laugh. "I was told my image could use a makeover."

"Ouch," Kelvin said as he followed Baxter into the change room. "Who dares to take the Great One's name in vain lately?"

"Apparently everyone on that great time suck called social media." He opened his locker and turned to face Kelvin. "No one pays any attention to that stuff. Do they?"

Kelvin shook his head in disbelief. "I guess that's what happens when your work day is all about make-believe."

"Really," Baxter persisted. "I'm not a bad guy."

"You're a successful, confirmed bachelor. Clearly straight. With no friends. It's bound to raise a few brows."

"I have lots of friends."

"You have lots of acquaintances. No friends that I'm aware of."

"Not even you?"

"The only reason you hang out with me is because I let you whale on me and vent your frustrations whenever the need arises. Which tends to be fairly often."

Baxter opened his mouth, but Kelvin raised a hand to silence him.

"How many guys do you know you can call up to go have a beer and shoot the shit with?"

Baxter was silent.

"How many people know what day your birthday is?" Kelvin continued. "Or invite you to have dinner at their place?" He waited expectantly.

Baxter remained stuck on the birthday question. "My brother knows my birthday." Or did he? Baxter was hard-pressed to remember that of his sibling.

"Does he call you on the day?"

Baxter looked down. He couldn't remember the last time he and Browning had spoken. It had been years and even then, something to do with their mother's long-term care. Nothing personal.

"Not even your mother?" Kelvin was watching him a little too closely for his liking.

"Poor woman doesn't even know her own name, let alone mine. Or the fact that she gave birth to me."

Kelvin clapped him on the shoulder. "Sorry I brought it up, man. It must have been hard, moving all the time when you were a kid."

Baxter tensed. "How'd you know that?"

"Social media. I look up everyone new when they join the gym."

Baxter's jaw dropped.

"And anyone who shows up as a Tinder match. Doctors,

lawyers, Indian Chief, whoever I have any dealings with. Don't you?"

Baxter shook his head. "Someone else does all that when we're casting or hiring crew."

Kelvin gave a knowing nod. "Someone tells you your image needs a makeover you'd be smart to listen."

BAXTER CLOSED his laptop and sat back in his chair. No friends, but lots of enemies it seemed, showing up on whatever media accounts he'd set up under protest years ago, prodded by a long-gone publicist when he was just starting his career. If his computer hadn't saved his various passwords, he'd not know the accounts were out there in cyberspace.

He'd never thought of himself as Mr. Congeniality, and apparently neither did most of the women who'd passed through his life over the years. He didn't remember most of them but it seemed they remembered him, and not exactly in glowing terms.

On impulse, he reached for his phone and dialed April Thomas. She answered on the first ring.

"How are things coming with the shine up Baxter Reid's image campaign?"

"Hello, Baxter. I'm fine, thank you. You?"

He huffed out a breath. "Not very popular from what I've been reading."

"I thought you stayed away from social media."

"Let's just say my curiosity was piqued."

Silence filled the airwaves. Finally she spoke. "Would you hire you?" He heard the other question in her voice.

What had happened to shift his original resistance to using her services?

"Listen, I know I gave you a bit of a hard time when we met. I've had some time to consider what you said and—"

"Did Mike threaten you?"

"Mike? No, why?"

"He predicted this would happen. That you'd come around."

Baxter didn't like the sound of that. He didn't like people knowing him better than he knew himself. Of course, when it came down to it, how well *did* he know himself? He'd bet Kelvin had no idea that his deadliest punch of the evening had been delivered when they weren't in the ring.

"I wouldn't care if it wasn't for that show. I don't give a rat's ass what John Q Public thinks of me. Too many people out there believe life is some sort of popularity contest."

"Don't count me in that camp," April said. "A lot of people create a fancy façade but anyone who matters can see right through it to the person's inner truth. Which in your case is exactly what we need to project. No glitz and glamor. Genuine truth."

"What's your façade?" he asked, suddenly curious.

"Oh, no you don't. This is project Baxter. Don't try to deflect things away from you and over to me."

"Why not?" Darned if he wasn't enjoying himself. When had he last enjoyed sparring with a woman?

Her voice had that low, tingly pitch that sent ripples of reaction up and down his spine. "It doesn't work that way."

"I'll show you my façade if you show me yours." He punctuated his words with a throaty chuckle that usually sent women rushing into his arms and his bed.

She cleared her throat pointedly. "When's the last time

you hired a woman as a stunt double? Even when the lead actress is a woman?"

"There's not a lot of women in the industry."

"That doesn't answer my question."

"I hire the best person for the job, regardless of gender."

"Because you believe the best person is a man."

He didn't appreciate having to justify his decisions. Maybe this image makeover was a bad idea. Maybe he didn't want the project this bad.

"Hit a nerve, did I?" she asked, breaking the lengthy silence between them.

He didn't ask how she knew.

Her voice softened. "This is something we ought to discuss in person."

Baxter heard himself agreeing to meet her the following day, even though whatever she had to say wasn't anything he wanted to think about, let alone discuss. Resolutely he picked up next week's shooting schedule. And thought about Kelvin asking if he had anyone to go grab a beer with. The guys he knew were all married, or at least coupled-up, which didn't mean he couldn't go to a bar by himself on Friday night. LA was overrun with pretty wannabe actresses happy to spend a few hours in the company of a film director.

CHAPTER 3

This time the town car purred to a stop just outside his building. She hadn't asked for his address, just told him to be ready and waiting at a pre-arranged time. No woman had ever dictated terms to him before; it had always been him calling the shots and he preferred it that way.

Once in the car, he sat back and crossed his arms over his chest.

"I'm here," he said grumpily, "as per your instructions."

She nodded. "I understand your discomfort. You're used to giving orders, not following them."

"Who says I'm uncomfortable?"

"Your body language for one thing. Your tone for another. Shall we go for three?"

"Let's just cut to the chase." He glanced out the window at the passing scenery, and noticed the city's skyline receding in the rearview mirror. "Where are we going?"

"You really like being in control, don't you? Is that because your father was in the military?"

Baxter leaned forward in exasperation. "I thought we were fixing my image, not dissecting my past."

"It's not a quick-fix. It's going to take time and patience on your part. We'll be spending a lot of time together over the next three or four months."

"Three or four *months*?" He didn't mean to raise his voice, but the thought of being shackled to this woman for months—

"As you are no doubt aware, MCU is still in negotiations for the live action rights to the characters."

"That's standard."

"It's also good news because it gives us time to do things right. By the time the rights are secured you will look like the golden boy, the only director who could possibly do the storyline and the character justice on the big screen."

He liked the sound of that. "Won't people talk if they see us together and figure out you're working with me?"

"Not if they think we're dating."

"Excuse me?"

Her lips twitched as if she was trying not laugh at his horrified expression.

"We'll be together in public a fair amount. It makes sense for people to think we're a couple. And having a steady girlfriend instead of a series of one-night stands can only help your reputation."

"My personal reputation is not under scrutiny."

"That's where you're wrong. You're known to be a staunch opponent of equality, diversity, matrimony, pretty much anything that ends with the letter Y."

"Not true. I just threw my buddy a stag party."

"Did a scantily-clad woman jump out of a cake?"

"Well—"

"You can't keep doing things like that, objectifying women that way."

"It's tradition," he mumbled staring down at his hands.

He felt her gaze on him and squirmed uncomfortably before he raised his eyes to meet hers.

"You know how they talk about politicians on the campaign trail, shaking hands and kissing babies?"

"I'm not on the campaign trail."

"What is this, if not your campaign to get a shot at directing *Sentry*?"

He didn't like admitting to her logic. "Am I going on tour with stops in key ridings?"

"In a manner of speaking."

He also didn't like the sound of that. "Am I being consulted? Or just told what to do?"

"Naturally, you're free to weigh in." She pulled out a tablet. "Mike gave me your upcoming shooting schedule—"

"Which is only a draft and subject to change."

"I've built in contingencies, but for now if you could please stick to the rough draft to the best of your ability it will be easier for both of us."

He propped his elbow on the car's window frame and stared out at the passing freeway, the cars rushing past them toward the Hollywood Hills. "Where are we going?"

"Laguna Beach."

Someplace he'd never been. "Why?"

"Why not?"

"I mean do you have me booked in to kiss some babies in a daycare or something?"

She laughed. "I'm waiting to hear back from Antman's agent as to his availability, but your first public appearance will be at the Children's Hospital in LA."

"I told you before, I don't like hospitals." He remembered going to see Blaze, a stuntman he'd worked with on a number of films, after a stunt went wrong and almost killed the guy. Blaze had been in the hospital for a wretchedly long time, and in rehab even longer. These days, his friend was walking proof that miracles do happen.

"Very few people do. But imagine if you're a kid who can't run and play and go to school like your friends."

He gave a mirthless laugh. "My brother and I never dared get sick. Our father considered illness a sign of weakness, and simply wouldn't allow it. I used to think Browning had asthma just to spite him." He bit off his words abruptly. Where had that come from? It wasn't something he was in the habit of sharing.

He saw a glimmer of something in her gaze that had better not be sympathy. "Didn't hurt us any. Made us stronger in the long run." Then he turned back to stare out the window. Before long, the ocean came into view. Then the town.

"WHERE WOULD you like me to drop you, miss?" the driver asked through the car's intercom.

"Anywhere on High Street where you can safely pull over," April said.

Minutes later the car idled to a stop and she and Baxter disembarked. Impossible to miss the way he stood stiffly on the sidewalk, hands stuffed into the pockets of his jeans and his shoulders hunched up around his ears. Yup, a man used to being in control of every situation wouldn't take kindly to today's outing. He actually looked as if someone had just dropped him on a foreign planet.

"What are we doing here?"

"I thought we'd poke through a couple of galleries, grab a bite, and then take a walk along the beach."

He shot her a suspicious look. "Why?"

"It's called getting to know each other. You should try it sometime. You might actually enjoy it."

"I don't think it's a good idea, you and me pretending to be an item. I mean who would believe it?"

"Right," April said. "Baxter Reid actually embarking on a relationship, first one of his lifetime. *Ever!*" She patted his shoulder. "I agree it will be a stretch, but do your best."

She reached the door of a nearby gallery, only to look over her shoulder and see him still standing where she'd left him. Slowly she returned to his side, their gazes colliding over the heads of passersby.

She stopped an arm's length away. He wore a little boy pout that reminded her of Liam.

"What do you mean, 'first relationship of my lifetime?' Emphasis on *ever*?"

"Hiring an agent is not a relationship. Hanging with the owner of a gym does not constitute a relationship. A brother you haven't communicated with in years. A mother you never visit. A series of one-night stands."

"And out-of-the-blue I'm supposed to fall for you?"

"And much like Ebeneezer Scrooge after his visit from ghosts of his past, present, and future, wake up a changed man. I can't honestly think of any other credible way to improve your image."

He gave a rueful smile. "You really go out of the way for your clients, don't you?"

"Let's just say I hate to lose." She paused before she continued. "You would not believe the people whose social standing has benefited from my work behind the scenes. And not just in the entertainment industry."

"Like who?"

She shook her head. "Classified information. Just allow

me to say it has been accomplished so seamlessly, no one even knows I had anything to do with it."

"Did you fake date them all?"

"Not a one."

"Then why me this time?"

She took a step forward and tucked her arm deliberately through his. "Let's just say I can't resist your charm." This time when she started toward the gallery, he had no choice but to go with her.

She didn't tell him the whole story. How she'd almost turned Mike down when he first brought up Baxter as a client. She wasn't even sure that someone so arrogant deserved a makeover. Let him reap what he sowed. Then she took a good dive below the surface and something she saw there struck a chord. It was obvious Baxter was his own worst enemy, his own saboteur, pretending not to care about anything or anyone besides his career.

April was tops in her field because of her ability to look past the façade and find redeeming traits that others over-looked. She had no doubt Baxter would be a challenge. His ego would be in the way every step. But she firmly believed she'd glimpsed things about the man that he, himself, wasn't aware of. Or if he were aware, would never admit to. Things like low self-esteem. Lack of self-worth. The need to prove something to himself as well as the rest of the world.

"Have you been to Laguna before?"

"Nope," he said. "No reason to."

"I love it," she said. "I treat myself to a weekend here from time to time, just to get out of the city, to unplug and recharge." She could tell from his blank look that he had no idea what she was talking about.

As she browsed through the gallery's selection of artisan gifts, jewelry, sculptures and paintings, her attention was caught by a dainty, brightly colored hummingbird in midflight, hanging by a length of fishing line from a tree made of driftwood.

She turned to Baxter, who appeared perplexed, as if he didn't know what to look at or why. How sad. On impulse she beckoned him over. "See this?" She drew his attention to the hummingbird.

"Yeah?"

"Can you buy this for me, please?"

He stared at her in disbelief. "What's the matter? Can't you afford it?"

She unhooked the object under discussion from the tree and placed it in his hand. "Careful, it's delicate," she said, almost feeling sorry for the colorful bird trapped in his huge, mitt-like hand.

"You want me to buy this for you?" He stared at the creature he held as if not quite sure how it got there.

"Uh, huh. And one day in the not-too-distant future its picture will show up on my social media accounts with a gushing remark of how you couldn't resist it, saying it reminded you of me."

"And people will believe that nonsense?"

She steered him toward the cashier. "Trust me. It's tiny things like that which will slowly sway public opinion from their preconceived notion of you toward the direction we want."

As Baxter tapped the payment terminal, the sales person showed them how each wing came out of the body for easy transport and promised to have the tiny creature wrapped and ready for them in an hour. April snapped a picture of the hummer with her phone so she'd know the right order to put the wings back in.

"I might need your help, sweetheart," she said with a

dazzling smile at Baxter for the clerk's sake. She doubted the woman knew Baxter was one of Hollywood's most successful directors, but it was clear from her coy looks and flirty actions she was taken by to his striking good looks and killer body.

"We'll be back in an hour or two," April said sweetly, tucking her hand back into the crook of Baxter's elbow, her hips swaying against his as they left the shop.

Outside, the town was bustling. She heard live music coming from a restaurant courtyard as they dodged numerous baby strollers, pedestrians, face-painting booths and a mime dressed like a mermaid. A block ahead, a small crowd was gathered around an acrobat duo.

"You look like you've accidently fallen down Alice's rabbit hole," she said teasingly.

"Is this what people do on a Saturday? Wander aimlessly, doing nothing?"

"Baxter, they're enjoying life. It's a beautiful sunny Saturday afternoon. There's art, there's music, there's laughter and entertainment."

"Seems like a giant waste of time."

"Some people feel that way about watching a film, let alone making one. Think of life as one big stage full of improv actors."

"I'd fire the lot of them," he mumbled. But she saw his shoulders relax and his mouth lose its pinched expression.

The next block over they smelled frying onions and passed a food truck dishing up pizza and tacos. April's feet stopped of their own accord, her stomach rumbling. She looked at Baxter. "Hungry?"

His expression was almost comical. "Looks like something the caterers serve on set every day."

"I guarantee, whatever the catering company makes for

the masses won't taste anything like this. Come on, my treat." Minutes later she accepted two recyclable food packets and joined Baxter where she'd parked him at a picnic table nearby. He accepted his taco, unwrapped one end and took a bite. She watched the way his chewing slowed down after the first bite, as if he was taking the time to actually enjoy the food. "Good?" she prompted between her own dainty nibbles, making sure not to spill on her sweater.

"Not bad," he said.

"What would you normally be doing on a Saturday?"

He shrugged. "Go to the gym. Grab a bite somewhere. Go home and watch the last week's rushes. Harass my AD's who are trying to spend time with their families with copious emails and phone calls. Pick up my laundry. See what's on the Sports channel. Guy stuff."

"Oh, yeah, guy stuff." Once her taco was finished, she gathered up her empty food wrapper and lobbed it in a nearby trash container.

"You?"

"I might spend part of the day working and tidying my place. Then I'd meet a friend to do something. Or if I didn't have plans, maybe I'd read or work in the garden."

"No man in your life?"

"Who says there isn't one?"

He raised his brow. "Educated guess in light of our supposed upcoming relationship."

"I'm between boyfriends." Years between, but he didn't need to know that.

"No hankering after a white picket fence?"

She gave him an exasperated look. "You need to drop that whole attitude."

"What attitude?"

"That all women want is to get married and have babies. If that's a legacy from your father based on the way he treated your mother, it's outdated."

"Leave my father out of this."

April nodded, watching him closely. She needed to earn his trust not antagonize him. "Your turn to choose the topic."

His entire body seemed to snap to attention. Much more comfortable when he was guiding the topic. "Let's talk about your family for a change. After all, it's your idea we get to know each other." He narrowed his gaze as if trying to X-ray her brain. "You're the oldest child, but your parents secretly wanted a boy. You're bossy. You probably got stuck looking after the younger kids a lot. Your mother was a stand-in for Betty Crocker. Your father was the disciplinarian, the little time that he was home."

She stood up. "Way off the mark. Let's go pick up my hummingbird and head for the beach."

CHAPTER 4

B axter was relieved to get back to work, back where things were sane and normal and somewhat predictable. Sure there were always surprises and glitches, but nothing he couldn't deal with. In fact, he thrived on the challenges of the industry. Temperamental actors. Equipment failures. Scheduling delays. Things he could meet head on and master. Admitting to feeling relaxed and refreshed after his day away from the city totally freaked him out.

Same as being with April Thomas. He never knew what to expect. Once they reached the beach, she'd kicked off her sandals and strolled along the water's edge, stopping occasionally to pick up an interesting shell or rock before carefully putting it back. Baxter was used to having a destination. A schedule. To move with purpose. This aimless wandering along the beach with the waves crashing into shore and seagulls screaming overhead took getting used to. But eventually his thoughts quieted and he let the surroundings saturate his senses.

At one point the breeze tangled April's skirt up around

her thighs and he realized she had really long legs. Nice legs. A nice figure too, for that matter. Nothing showy, but curves in all the right places. He was so used to being surrounded by fake tits that he found the slight jiggle of her breasts as she moved intriguing, and wondered what kind of bra she wore.

As he pulled his attention from thoughts of April's lingerie to the matters at hand, the lighting tech working his magic to make the set even moodier, his phone buzzed. April's number. He frowned. As if she'd known he was thinking about her. Which was not possible.

She confirmed two of the events they'd talked about on the way back to LA from Laguna. A hospital visit Friday after work and a black-tie event Saturday night. He hadn't told her about his friend's upcoming wedding. Or his crazy middle-of-the-night idea to take her along as his 'plus one.'

He frowned as the stunt coordinator set up a shot. The show's lead actor was a female, yet as they started to shoot this scene it seemed obvious to him that her stunt double was a man. Things like that had never bothered him before April brought it up. He yelled "Cut!" and went into a huddle with Alonzo, the stunt coordinator.

"Can't you make him move more like a woman?" he asked.

"Like a woman?"

"You know softer. Gentler. Rounder." The poor guy looked at him like he was crazy. And maybe he was.

WHEN APRIL'S town car rolled up to the curb he stepped inside eagerly, deflated to see the back seat was empty. His disappointment must have been visible in the vehicle's interior light before he slammed the door and the light went out.

"Miss Thomas will meet you at the hospital, sir."

"Very good."

At least he didn't have to spend a couple of hours in make-up and costume the way Paul did for this visit. Still, it would be nice to see the enigmatic actor again. He wondered why, once a show wrapped, he never saw any of the cast or crew again. Not unless they ended up together on a new project. People he'd worked with were pleasant enough if their paths happened to cross his, but only in a superficial way. LA. Land of make believe and superficiality. Exception, April Thomas. Spending the day with her led him to believe she was the real deal.

As the driver let him off outside the hospital's main entrance, Baxter figured there was something to be said for not scrambling to find parking. The automatic doors whished open to a lobby that was unexpectedly crowded, abuzz with anticipation. He looked over the heads of staff, patients and visitors milling about and finally spotted April. Then he blanched. A reporter and cameraman from KTLA were trailing behind her. Why hadn't she warned him the press would be here? He'd never been a media darling, and the press tended to treat him as if he was a hostile witness.

"There you are, sweetheart." She took his hand and gave him a peck on the cheek. He took advantage of her proximity to pull her close and speak directly in her ear. "Why didn't you tell me the press would be here?"

"The element of surprise. It has to look spontaneous, not staged."

He forced a smile, aware he was being scrutinized as he stepped back a pace, their still-joined hands swinging between them. "I'll get you for this," he said through his smile, his words too low to be heard by anyone other than her.

The focus shifted abruptly with Paul's arrival. The press loved Paul. Meanwhile, April was leading him toward a woman in a hospital uniform carrying a clipboard. "Theresa is a child life specialist who coordinates celebrity visits for the children."

The woman's handshake was brisk and business-like. "A pleasure to meet you, Mr. Reid. You have a lot of fans among our patients."

"That's kind of you to say so." He inclined his head in Paul's direction. "I know who the real star is."

"You're too modest," April said. "You know you can hold your own. After all, without your skills, there wouldn't be a movie."

"The real credit goes to the writers who created Antman and his fellow Superheroes in the first place." Listening to himself, Baxter felt someone else was putting words in his mouth. When had he sounded either smooth or modest?

"If you're ready?" Theresa said, heading for the elevators where Paul stood waiting amidst a gaggle of media types.

As April's fingers linked through his, he was glad she was there.

"First hospital visit, Mr. Reid?" asked one reporter.

"No," Baxter said, "but it's my first one with Paul as my wingman." He gave the man his best smile. "I'm better behind the camera than in front of it."

When the elevator arrived, Theresa whisked them in quickly and closed the door on the press. "There are a few things we like to cover with all of our special visitors," she said as the elevator started to rise, "to help things go smoothly for you and our patients. Although they seem like natural questions, we request that you don't ask about why the kids are in the hospital, or their illness. Similarly, saying you hope they feel better soon or get to go home soon, are also potentially upsetting comments best avoided."

Oh, God! This was going to be a minefield, where any innocent comment could make a child cry. Baxter was bound to mess up. He could see the headlines now: 'Antman Director Upsets Entire Children's Hospital'. This wasn't even his idea to start with.

"The kids are excited to see you, but they're also nervous and may turn shy. It's a good idea to have some safe questions at the ready. Asking who their favorite Superhero is, or what animal they wish they could communicate with the way Antman does, are good examples. What's their favorite movie. That kind of thing. We want to keep this visit fun and positive." Her gaze met his squarely.

Was his dislike of hospitals obvious?

"Just remember, children are children, inside these walls or out. If you're friendly, they'll warm up to you." She smiled, seeming far more confident in his ability to engage with the patients than he was. The elevator doors opened and they stepped onto the ward.

Baxter wrinkled his nose. There it was! That smell. Heavy cleaner. Stale air. Sickness. His grip on April's hand tightened and she shot him a questioning look. "Have you done this before?" he asked.

April nodded as they followed Theresa's straight back down the hall.

"And?" Baxter said.

"Remember what Theresa said. Kids are kids."

Paul followed them through a doorway at the end of the hall and into a room that was not at all what Baxter expected. He'd been anticipating a hospital room with a couple of patients. Instead, they were in a large, bright room, two walls covered floor to ceiling with shelves of toys. The room was jammed not just by kids, but a number of adults milled around as well. He was surprised to see some of the young-sters wearing street clothes. But the rest— He hadn't been prepared for the sight of wheelchairs, IV poles, NG tubes.

The second they entered, the room fell silent and he and Paul became the subject of dozens of pairs of expectant eyes. April abandoned him, sliding off to stand at the back of the room.

"Didn't I tell you Antman and Mr. Reid would be here soon?" Theresa said. Heads nodded.

"I thought Antman would be tiny," said a thin young boy in a wheelchair near the front.

Paul looked at Baxter. "That's a trick they do with the special effects. Baxter can tell you how."

Except he couldn't. He was a fraud. He had no business being here. "Well I could, but I can't," he said when the silence grew unbearable.

"Why not?"

Why not? Think!

"It's a secret. What if Egghead or Crossfire or Vespa happened to find out? Can you imagine?"

Silence returned. An IV tube started beeping some-where in the room. Someone coughed. He was really screwing this up. It seemed Paul wasn't much good without a script to memorize. In desperation, he looked around. At the back of the room, he spotted a huge poster covered in Antman's Supervillain enemies. He stalked in that general direction and pointed an accusing finger. "Who invited *them*?"

"They're not real," someone said.

"Phew!" He feigned relief. "That's good."

Theresa came to his rescue. "We'll be having a contest later. To see who can blast the most Supervillains with our super goo." She leaned toward him "AKA watered down paint," she said, in a voice only he could hear.

That's when he realized the wall behind the poster was draped with plastic, and a nearby table was piled with syringes filled with colored liquid. Okay, blasting Supervillains. Maybe this visit could be fun after all. Which was going to be up to him since Paul was standing still as a statue at the front, like he was some sort of mime.

"Who's your favorite Superhero?" Baxter asked. "Maybe I can make a movie about them next. Go ahead, who have you seen in the comics who deserves his own movie?"

An older girl at the back raised her hand. The other hand was attached to an IV pole. Her hair was chopped above her shoulders, shoe polish black on the bottom half and mousy brown at the top. Dark eyes in a pale face challenged his.

"Moon Dragon," she said.

"Moon Dragon," Baxter repeated. "What do you like about her?"

"Well, duh! She's a girl."

"Good point," Baxter said. "I guess a lot of the Superheroes are guys, aren't they?" He avoided looking at April as he spoke.

The girl made a scoffing expression. "It's obvious someone thinks only boys read comics or watch superhero movies. I mean look at the female costumes. Who are those for?"

Baxter was lost for words. The kid had a point.

Theresa took pity on him and stepped forward. "I bet a lot of the youngsters and their families would love to get their picture taken with Antman, or get his autograph. So while you're waiting your turn, line up to take down some of the Supervillains. Mr. Reid, why don't you go first? Normally you're the one who tells the Superheroes what to do. We'd all love to see how you do in the Superhero role yourself."

Baxter nodded. Suddenly he realized what the oversize picture on the far wall was for. Thomas the Tank Engine was super-sized so whoever stood in front of it looked tiny in comparison. Not quite ant-sized, but the idea was sound. And more creative than he would have come up with.

Someone, he assumed it was a volunteer, stepped up and guided him to the Supervillain poster and handed him one of the filled syringes. His effort was pathetic, not even hitting the poster. He heard jeers and laughter behind him from those waiting their turn. It was a humbling sound when so few of these kids had much to laugh about. Some would eventually go home. Others wouldn't.

A little girl wearing a hospital gown was next in line. She stepped up beside him and took his hand. "It's okay Mr. Reid, don't feel bad. You can try again. I bet you'll hit the target this time!" She handed him her syringe and smiled up at him, revealing a missing front tooth.

The jeers turned to cheers of encouragement. Baxter's heart felt funny, and it suddenly grew overly warm in the playroom. It seemed like the most natural thing in the world to kneel down so he was on the little girl's level. "What's your name?"

"Grace."

"Well Grace, do you think you could show me how?"

She nodded, then concentrating hard, the tip of her

tongue tucked in the corner of her mouth, she carefully positioned her hands on the syringe and squirted the paint. It was a direct hit on one of the characters on the poster.

A volunteer quickly handed them each a fresh syringe. "Why don't you two each take one more turn together."

Staying crouched down next to Grace, Baxter aimed his syringe.

"One, two..." Grace counted, "three!"

And they both hit the target, splattering paint. The volunteers, along with several kids waiting their turn, clapped and cheered. When Grace turned and beamed at him, Baxter felt like a Superhero.

"We make a good team! Thanks for showing me how, Grace." He held his hand up, palm out, and received a high five.

Baxter straightened and stepped back, aware of Paul posing across the room while his competitors did a much better job with the syringe than him. They were no doubt used to syringes. Used to a lot of hospital paraphernalia that had no business being part of their young lives, and with sudden insight, he realized what the activity was doing. Allowing kids to have fun with medical equipment that was normally associated with less pleasant parts of their hospital stay. And putting them in control. Smart. He could have used someone like Theresa making the hospital a less frightening place to visit when he was younger.

A boy of about ten approached with his iPad. He showed Baxter a stop-motion movie he'd been filming with his Star Wars Lego. It was actually very clever, and the boy seemed delighted by Baxter's praise.

"Did you hear?" the boy said to his mom as they walked away. "A real director liked my movie!"

A real director! Still smiling from that comment, he

noticed a girl, probably on the cusp of her teenage years, standing alone as she watched the photo shoot from a distance. She was wearing ripped-up jeans and a faded hoodie, so not a patient. He sidled over to her. "You waiting to get a picture?"

She shrugged one thin shoulder. "Probably not."

"Why not?"

She huffed out a weighty sigh that made her sound far older than her years. "I don't need a picture. My parents are up there with my sister. It's kids like her and," she gestured with her arm, indicating the other patients. "They're the ones who need the pictures with the celebrity visitors."

Oh. No doubt the parents were so wrapped up with the sick kid, understandable really, this was something no parent should have to go through but—

He flashed back to his own childhood. His brother hadn't been sick, that had been their mother, but Browning had asthma and allergies and always seemed to be the sole focus of their parents' attention. "Let's us go," he said abruptly.

At her surprised look, he said, "You and me and Antman can get our picture taken together."

"Just us?" She glanced at him shyly. "Can I post it on Snapchat? My friends won't believe who I met!"

"Sure. Come on. You got your phone?" As he steered the girl past April, he caught her eye and warmed at the approving look she sent him. Maybe he wasn't such a dud at this stuff after all.

After his photo op, the rest of the time passed in a blur. He saw parents overwhelmed with joy when Paul signed a glossy publicity photo with their kid's name. He overheard a teary mom tell a nurse this was the first time she'd seen her son smile and act like himself since his surgery.

Near the end of the visit, he and Paul had a shootout on the villain board, each with a patient team cheering them on. Paul's team was larger, but Baxter was touched he had some fans on his side too. The boy who had shown him his Lego movie, and the teenage girl he took his first photo with were on his side rooting for him. And Grace, his syringe paint instructor, stood at the front and cheered the loudest.

"Tonight's visit should be on the eleven o'clock news," April said as the three of them spilled into the waiting town car. "You were great, both of you."

Baxter thought 'great' was a stretch. But he had been surprised at how well the event had gone after his initial fumbling. It was hard to pretend he wasn't mad at a world where innocent children were victims of accidents and disease. The pain, the procedures, an uncertain future where some of them were terminal. Despite that, all of them were full of smiles and laughter, and he'd found himself at a loss for words more than once. He'd forgotten about the press, the show he was working on, the story he had his sights set on.

"You know man," Paul said. "Those kids tonight, those are the true heroes."

Baxter nodded. He couldn't have said it better. Impulsively he turned to April. "There must more we can do for them? Or for their families?"

She stared at him as if seeing him for the first time. "There are many worthwhile fundraisers you can support throughout the year. But they're not the only worthy cause. You're going to attend another one tomorrow."

Right, tomorrow. He'd better pick up his tux from the cleaner's first thing.

APRIL'S PHONE buzzed letting her know her car was out front. She picked up her evening bag and wrap. What to wear had been a toss-up between the teal gown or the claret one; eventually she'd chosen the claret, hoping it was true that red was a power color; something she needed around Baxter. Both gowns had been designed to impart the perfect balance of power and femininity, making the most of her physical assets without giving too much away.

She gave Robert, her driver, Baxter's address for his GPS and checked the contents of her evening bag. Lipstick, tissue, phone, pepper spray, credit card and cash. She closed the clasp and sat back. She couldn't think of a better cause for tonight's fundraiser than the Global fund for Women and its gender justice movements to empower women around the globe.

Baxter had obviously been impacted by yesterday's hospital visit, and the late-night news snip had been favorable. Tonight, she hoped he gained insight into some of the injustices women were dealt. Hopefully, that would have an impact as well.

She'd never fake-dated a client before and was still questioning the wisdom of her decision, but after examining the situation from every angle she honestly hadn't seen any other way. Her family would be delighted, until they learned the truth. No one said so out loud, but they'd been worried about her ever since that night— She pushed the memory away.

By now, Baxter would have heard the news that MCU had given the green light for *Sentry* to be made into a feature-length film and were looking at writers. She was curious about his reaction. Would he show up with renewed determination? Would he accept that she knew what she was doing and go along with future suggestions? She sensed that Baxter rarely willing went along with much unless the idea originated with him first.

"Did you hear?" They were the first words out of his mouth when he got in the car.

"About *Sentry*? Yes, I did."

"You had better know your stuff."

She gave him a cold look. "Any reason so far to think I don't "know my stuff"?

"Sorry." He slouched against his seat back. "I hate when things are dependent on the whims of others."

"So I gathered." She could sympathize. Almost. It was the one thing they had in common. "Did you catch last night's news?"

"Mike was thrilled."

Hmmph. No mention of how Baxter felt. Could it be the hospital visit had triggered feelings he also wasn't able to control?

He seemed to see her for the first time. "You look nice."

"Thank you. Is that Armani?"

He gave a curt nod. Silence stretched between them. "How's the hummingbird?"

She started at the question, then realized he was refer-ring to the one they'd bought at the gallery in Laguna. "I managed to put it back together," she said. "I'm still looking for the right spot to display it."

He seemed to take that in, as if he knew art needed to be displayed in the right place. "How am I supposed to act tonight?"

"Just be yourself."

He shot her a look. "We both know 'myself' is not a person who would normally be attending a women's fundraiser."

"Think of it as something the 'new you' would do. Aiding the empowerment of women."

He quirked a brow as if he found the idea amusing. "Gender equality."

She stayed silent, waiting for him to say more.

He splayed his hands flat on the car seat. He had big hands, strong and capable looking with masculine, well-kept nails. "Everyone knows women are superior. They live longer, have a higher threshold for pain, are emotionally stronger and generally less combative than men. Unfortunately, women will never best men when it comes to sheer physical strength. There is a different genetic makeup and hormonal balance at play." He leaned closer. "Our bodies are designed to fulfill different tasks in society."

"I won't spout statistics about how difficult it has been in the past for women to get an education, take up a trade, become accepted in the political ring or receive equal pay for equal work."

"That tide is turning. Slowly I admit, but things are moving in the right direction."

"It's up to you to walk that talk."

"By hiring an all-women crew for my films?"

"It'll take a whole lot more than that."

"Just promise you won't try to turn me into a male Kardashian."

She choked back a laugh at the absurdity of such a thing. "Last thing on my mind." She sobered. "Yesterday at the hospital, that wasn't an act with you. You were truly genuine. The press recognized that and responded accordingly."

When the car pulled up outside the hotel where the event was taking place, he got out first and turned to help her. "Never let it be said I won't do whatever it takes to land *Sentry*. Even pretend to fall for you."

"I'll try not to make it too difficult."

He tucked her free hand protectively in the crook of his elbow as they headed for the door. "This I have to see."

CHAPTER 5

April had to hand it to Baxter. He could be charming when he wanted to. Right now, he was off bidding up a storm on the silent auction items and Lillian slid into his empty seat.

"When you told me you were bringing Baxter Reid, the director, tonight I googled him and wondered what you were doing with a man like that. But he's nothing at all the way the media paints him."

"I know," April said. "He was all gruff arrogance when we met. Turned out to be an act. He thought he needed to act that way to earn the respect of his peers. Seems they like the real him a lot better. Everyone does."

Lillian glanced across the room. "Looks like Needy Nellie has him in her sights."

April bit her lip in amusement. She'd met Nellie before, a much-acclaimed blogger and social media influencer who liked to be in first with the latest LA gossip. The nickname fit. Still, a positive word from her could go a long way to painting Baxter as having turned over a new leaf. The pair were coming this way.

"Gotta scoot," Lillian said. "I've already had my coal-raking with her earlier."

"April," Nellie said, as the pair approached the table. "You could have knocked me over with a feather when I saw Baxter here, never mind when he told me who his date was."

April rose and went to Baxter, tucking her arm around his waist. His arm settled possessively on her shoulder. "Did you convince him not to buy out the entire auction table, Nell? I told him to leave something for the other guests to bid on."

"I don't think anyone can dissuade Baxter once he has his mind set a certain way." She cocked her head and studied them like a bird sizing up a worm. "So interesting to see the two of you together. He tells me you're attending a wedding with him next weekend in Washington state."

April tried to hide her surprise. First she'd heard about it. "Oh, did he now?"

"Yes. I confess to a faint twinge of jealousy. I adore the Pacific Northwest this time of year. Don't you?"

Baxter put a teasing finger to his lips as if sharing a secret. "April favors Laguna Beach, but I intend to sway her toward the appeal of the Oregon and Washington coast. Far less crowded."

"Mercy, yes," Nellie said. "It will be a wonderful getaway for the two of you. What was the name of the Island again? I must look it up."

"Blue Sky Island. Just far enough from the mainland to have its own unique charm, but close enough that its residents can still work in the city."

"Well, you both have a wonderful time. It's been a pleasure chatting with you." With a girlish wave, Nellie sailed through the crowd, looking for her next victim.

"That went well," Baxter said.

"You didn't mention *Sentry*, I hope."

He shook his head. "I told her I was looking at several projects and one in particular had caught my attention recently, but that's all."

"Good. I wasn't sure you could handle subtle, but that's how this campaign has to play."

Before long the meal was served, typical hotel fare, followed by the predictable speeches and PowerPoint presentations.

"How did you land up with this lot?" Baxter asked her, as the auctioneer was getting set up for the live auction.

"They've recently asked me to sit on the Board,"

"And will you?"

"I'm making the time. They do some very impressive work worldwide."

"And that's important to you?"

"Despite what people might think, the Universe doesn't stop and start at the freeway entrance to LA." She turned to him. "Who's getting married?"

"A buddy of mine."

"It would have been nice to be asked, not have it sprung on me like that."

"That works both ways," Baxter said before he turned his attention back to the action on stage.

"What have I sprung on you?"

He turned his head and sent her a laconic look.

"I mean it," she said. "What?"

He leaned so close she could feel his breath tickling her ear. "Suddenly, I not only have a media makeover, I have a girlfriend. At least, so people are being led to believe."

He had her there.

APRIL'S PHONE rang just as she was leaving her self-defense course. She answered as she got into the waiting car.

"Hey, Mackenzie."

"Hi, Sis." Mackenzie sounded hesitant, which was very un-Mackenzie like. "Whatcha up to?"

"Just finished my self-defense class."

"You're still doing that?"

"Yes, and I plan to continue for the foreseeable future."

Hollow laugh. "Haven't you trained enough to take down anyone who dares get in your way?"

April didn't answer. She knew her family considered it high time she got over that fateful night years ago when she had been car-jacked and attacked.

"What is it you want, Mac?" Sad, but true, Mackenzie never called her without asking for something, whether it was a loan, a reference letter, or more recently, childcare.

"I wondered if there was any chance of you looking after Liam one day next weekend."

"Sorry," April said absently. "I won't be here." She'd resolutely cleared her mind for her lesson and now that it was over, her thoughts drifted back to last night's fundraising dinner and Baxter's roundabout invitation to his friend's wedding. She was as bad as him, always wanting to be the one who called the shots, but he'd caught her short.

Baxter had been top bid for several auction items and when he was called on stage to make arrangements for pick up, he had generously donated everything back to the charity to use as they saw fit. It was an unprecedented move that garnered him a slew of gratitude and respect. Including from her. It was also a bold move, bound to spark a fair amount of buzz among the movers and shakers who had been in attendance. She almost wished she'd thought of it herself, and wondered how Nellie would handle it in her blog, Petranella's People. No one expressed any interest in the blog, but everyone she knew read it fanatically.

"You never go away on the weekend," Mackenzie said, almost as if she suspected April of fabricating an excuse.

"I guess that makes the upcoming weekend an exception."

"Work or pleasure?"

April gave a short laugh. "Work of course. That seems to be my life these days."

"Is Baxter Reid included under the work column?"

"What do you mean?"

"There's a rumor that you and him are suddenly an item. I didn't believe it, of course. He's not even close to being your type."

What was her type?

"I wasn't aware you and Baxter were acquainted."

There was a slight hesitation on the other end. "We went out once, years ago."

"You never mentioned him before."

"Nothing worth mentioning."

"How many years ago?" April asked, a sudden, suspicious thought niggling at her. Mackenzie had never revealed the identity of Liam's father. Surely—

"Oh, I don't remember," Mackenzie said offhandedly. "So where are you off to?"

"A small island off the coast of Washington."

She heard Mackenzie's gasp. "So it *is* true? You and Baxter are going to Blaze's wedding. Together." Before she could confirm or deny, Mackenzie continued. "Good thing for your self-defense training. You'll need it." Then she hung up.

April sat staring at her phone for several long, thoughtful minutes before she looked up Nellie's blog post.

It featured a candid photo of her and Baxter where they appeared to be gazing at each other with undisguised interest.

"It seems Hollywood's notorious bad-boy director is turning over a new leaf, thanks in part, I'm sure to what some might speculate to be 'more than friendship' with Revitalique's April Thomas. I wasn't the only one surprised to see Baxter Reid at the Global Fund for Women's fundraising gala. You had to be there to catch the ripple of disbelief, for the director is not exactly renowned for his equal opportunity for women in film attitude. However, to his credit, not only did Reid attend the event, he bought out the silent auction items and donated them back to the Global Fund. Quite an about-face for a man known for his, shall we speak candidly between us, somewhat cavalier attitude toward others."

At least it was a decent photo, not quite in your face coupledom, but hinting at enough chemistry to beg the question 'are they or are they not together?'. Not that any suggestion of chemistry was real. Baxter Reid was just another job. So why didn't she feel a sense of accomplishment? After all, this was exactly what she'd been hired to do.

BAXTER HAD JUST REACHED his car on the studio lot when Mike pulled up alongside him. "Get in."

Baxter eyed his agent with distrust. Mike was a bulldog, which is why Baxter had signed with him in the first place, but lately he was questioning some of the agent's tactics. "I'm late for the gym."

"You'll want to hear this."

It was too soon for any word on *Sentry*. And he couldn't

imagine what else would warrant a personal visit. He reluctantly opened the passenger door of Mike's vintage Thunderbird convertible and got in. "Something wrong with the phone?"

With the car idling, Mike turned and rested one arm on the seat back as he faced Baxter. "Good news needs to be shared in person. My inside sources tell me the studio seems to be warming slightly to you."

Baxter made a scoffing noise. "That's your big news? They don't even have a script yet."

"Don't be so sure about that. Anyway, two weeks ago, you were persona non grata. Anyone who dared mention your name would have been shut down."

Baxter never knew when Mike was being straight with him or pulling his leg. "So no meeting as of yet?"

"It's too soon for that. The deal hasn't formally been inked, which means everything out there is still in the rumor stage. Those guys have a lot of other irons in the fire."

Baxter crossed his arms over his chest. "I've got my own irons heating up."

Mike's expression grew thoughtful. "As long as one of them isn't April Thomas. Don't toy with her, Baxter."

Baxter stiffened. "You're the one who siced her on me. Or have you forgotten this was all your idea?"

"Despite your reputation for being an unfeeling SOB where the fairer sex is concerned."

"A reputation I did nothing to deserve, I might add."

"Except not care about anyone besides yourself." Mike blew out a breath. "April's good people. She gives every client more than one hundred percent. The problem for people who work that way is they keep nothing back for themselves." He pressed his lips together. "Know why she doesn't drive herself at night, ever?"

"Issues with her night vision?"

Mike shook his head. "It's not common knowledge, I only know because I know one of her brothers, half or step or whatever he is to her, I can never keep it sorted. Some years back she was car-jacked one night, attacked and held hostage. The experience made her wary. She didn't quit working but she's very selective about her clients. She gave up her office downtown. She uses the town car and driver anytime she meets her clients, the same driver she's had for years."

"She distrusts men?"

"Not all men. But you have to earn her trust."

"Why are you telling me this?"

"I read Nellie's blog, and I know you plan to fly up there. Somehow, I doubt she expects it will be just the two of you, alone in your plane. I'm not sure how she'll react when she finds out, but you need to be sensitive to what happened to her before."

Baxter fell silent. So, April Thomas was wary around men. Which meant it was up to him to allay any fears she might have about being alone with him.

CHAPTER 6

April's thoughts kept circling back to a throwaway remark Baxter made on the trip to Laguna. Something about how neither he or his brother dared get sick. A statement which told her more than he said. How their father had been a hard task master, which went hand in hand with the military background.

Most of her clients came to her directly, offering full disclosure about their backgrounds, grateful for her help. Baxter was the exception, and since digging into people's backgrounds was beyond her paygrade or comfort zone, she'd hired a professional. As she went over his findings, she felt a little guilty prying into a past Baxter preferred stay buried.

The investigator's report painted a picture of a young boy who never felt he measured up to his father's exacting standards. It made sense that was the way he now treated others, which gained him a fair bit of resentment judging by the posts slagging him and his unreasonable expectations. Baxter had been the most robust of the two sons, the one who fell victim to his father's disciplinary actions more than the younger boy, whom she learned had spent time in the hospital with severe allergies and asthma.

Apparently, the father's authoritarian ways proved too much for the boys' mother who sunk first into bouts of depression, followed by early-onset Alzheimer's. Ironically, she outlived the father and was still alive in an expensive care home. Baxter footed the bill.

She stared out the window, momentarily distracted by the movement of the bright pink bougainvillea as a slight breeze blew through the yard. What if Baxter wasn't so much disdainful of women as intimidated by everything he didn't know about them, having grown up in a predominantly male household? That would certainly paint a different picture of Baxter than the man the media knew.

She sighed. None of this was much help. No way would Baxter sit still for a wave of public sympathy. She was better off staying with her original plan before she knew much about his background. To slowly shift the public's perception of him. He'd never be the best-friend-boy-next-door type, but he could become known as the guy you could depend on in a pinch. The guy with others' best interests at heart.

Just then her phone rang. She stared at the screen. Think of the devil and who should call?

"You eat yet?"

"I beg your pardon?"

"You know, lunch, that all-important midday meal."

"Aren't you on set with your artery-clogging catered meals?"

"We wrapped yesterday. Now it's post production, but I try to take a little break before I switch gears. I just ordered a picnic."

April stared at the phone. Baxter. A picnic?

"I'm heading to Barnsdall Art Park. Meet me there?"

An art park? "I didn't know you had an interest in art."

"Architecture. Big fan of Frank Lloyd Wright. What do you say? Is it a date? You know, something spontaneous like a couple who are really dating would do. Or so I've been told."

"Give me an hour." She hung up, decidedly off-kilter. No way was Baxter about to think he could wrestle the control from her in this fake relationship. But she was too intrigued at the prospect of him planning a picnic not to show up.

BY THE TIME she reached the parking lot he'd texted her a picture of where he'd set up, complete with what looked suspiciously like a new plaid picnic blanket. Two colorful plates and glasses waited near a large wicker basket. It was an Insta-worthy shot which she saved on her phone's gallery.

He'd obviously been watching for her, for he sauntered toward her with a guileless smile that put her on guard. When he reached her side, he whipped a single long-stemmed rose from behind his back and presented it to her with a bow.

She gazed at its velvety yellow petals. "Who are you and what have you done with my surly and uncooperative client?"

"Like you predicted, old Ebeneezer and I have seen the error of our ways and woke up with a serious attitude adjustment."

"If this is a bid to tell me you no longer require my services—"

"Nothing of the sort. But we're going to a wedding. I can

hardly introduce you to everyone when I know next to nothing about you other than a soft spot for hummingbirds, Laguna Beach and deliciously messy tacos. You look nice, by the way."

"Thank you." He did too. In a pair of indigo jeans that loved his glutes and a white linen shirt with the sleeves rolled back. Mmmmm...forearms.

"What do you call this color?" He lightly caressed the sleeve of her silk blouse.

"Pistachio."

"How about that? My favorite flavor of ice cream."

She wasn't sure whether to believe him or not. She'd seen him at his charming best at the dinner the other night but it hadn't been directed full force at her, more like a wide-angle beam that encompassed everything and everyone. Today she felt the spotlight of his attention solely on her.

He took her free hand and led her to the blanket. "I wasn't sure what you like, so I got a bit of everything. Kind of a crash course to your likes and dislikes." He paused. "You're not on a restricted diet or anything are you? Allergies or—"

"I eat everything." She sat down slowly, tucking her legs under her while being careful not to kick anything over. There were even cloth napkins. He'd done all this to try to get to know her, while she'd resorted to hiring a background specialist. Now she really felt guilty. She blinked up at him. Or could he somehow have found out what she'd done? And was trying to manipulate her into—

Stop it! She'd spent her entire life feeling manipulated, trying to fit in, a round peg in the square hole that was her life.

She looked up to see him watching her with undisguised interest. "What?"

"I've heard the expression 'a myriad of expressions

crossed her face', but I've never seen it until just this second. And I'm not sure it's something I could coax out of the most skilled of actors."

She attempted to laugh it off. "I confess to being touched by your unexpected thoughtfulness."

He flashed her a grin. "See? Never believe everything you read about a person."

She stiffened. The person she'd hired to dig into his background had assured her it was impossible for the subject to find out. And yet such an abrupt about face on his part—

"It must be a relief when the filming is finished."

He laughed and reached for her plate. "Now the hard part starts. Turning thousands of takes into a film people will pay good money to watch."

He didn't ask permission to serve her, just delved into container after container and commenced loading her plate. Hard and soft cheeses with crusty slices of baguette. A variety of salads and cold meats. Pickles. Olives. Prawns. Dolmades. Scotch egg slices. Marinated artichoke hearts.

"Did you buy out the shop?" she asked in amusement when he finally passed her the plate and started on his own.

"What can I say? Everything looked good." After further rooting through the oversize hamper, he passed her a can of mineral water. "Bon appetit!"

She nibbled a wedge of cheese. He seemed different than the day they went to Laguna. More relaxed. Maybe he was getting used to her. Or maybe he really did wind down once a project reached the home stretch.

They ate in silence for a few minutes.

"I'll start," he said. "Some of this you already know. Younger brother I rarely see or speak with. No animosity there, just different guys with different lives and interests.

Single last I heard, no kids. Mother still alive, but not really here. Nasty disease, Alzheimer's. They say, as your days on earth reach the end, you at least have your memories. Sadly, she doesn't even have those."

She'd heard the disease was hereditary. He didn't strike her as the worrying type but maybe he was concerned it was in his DNA.

"Father deceased. Never knew any aunts, uncles or cousins. Not exactly a big warm, fuzzy family atmosphere. I'm sure a shrink would have a field day with all this." He sent her a self-deprecating smile.

She blotted her lips with the napkin and took a sip from her mineral water. "Have you ever been to see someone?"

"Never felt the need. Now to you. Favorite color?"

That stumped her. "Depends on my mood, I suppose."

"So that's how this goes," he said teasingly. "Lucky number?"

She quirked a brow. "Not asking my horoscope sign?"

He laughed aloud. "Sweetheart, I don't even know my own."

She narrowed her gaze. Taurus, she'd guess. Or maybe Leo with that thick mane of hair. Wait! Why was she noticing his hair and imagining how it would feel to run her hands through it? He gave her a faintly mocking smile, almost as if he knew what she was thinking.

"Back in Laguna I made a stab at guessing your background and you said I was way off the mark."

"Let me guess. You went home and asked Dr. Google about me."

He shook his head. "I thought I'd give this a try instead. Wine and dine you until you tell me all your deep, dark secrets from the past.

She rolled a couple of olives round on her plate. "Ever hear of the movie, *Yours, Mine and Ours?*"

"Doesn't sound like something on my radar."

"Mine either, but it kind of depicted my life, times two." She took a breath and launched into her carefully rehearsed speech when quizzed about her family. "After they got divorced, both my parents remarried someone who had kids already. Nothing unusual about that except they both went on to have more with their new partner."

He raised a brow, waiting for her to continue. "I have five step brothers and sisters and five half brothers and sisters. It's quite something when we all get together with their partners and kids."

"You must have to rent a hall."

"Pretty much. There's the usual discord, of course. I gave up long ago trying to keep up with who was mad at who over some slight, real or imagined." She pleated a corner of her napkin between her thumb and forefinger.

"Who'd you live with?"

"All of them. I moved back and forth every week."

"No wonder you're a control freak. You had zero control when you were young."

"I am not a control freak. I let you pick out the food and the venue today."

"Only because you didn't have a choice."

She leveled him a straight gaze. "I always have a choice." Her words came out more vehemently than she meant them to, but Baxter refrained from comment, diving back into his plate of food. She blew out a breath. How had he done that? Turned the tables and made her feel defensive about her past.

"I've been thinking. It's probably better if you go to the

wedding alone," she said, as she set her plate aside and stretched out her legs.

He raised his brow as if amused. "Not a chance. Blaze's fiancée read about us coming to their wedding together and he got heck for not telling her I was bringing a date. Now she's dying to meet you. Come on," he said. "Let's go walk off our lunch and you can tell me how to behave so people believe I'm your dream boyfriend."

April stood and brushed off her jeans. She had no more idea than Baxter did how her ideal boyfriend would act. All she knew was that there was no such animal.

BAXTER WAS RELIEVED when April's car and driver pulled up near his plane's hangar right on time. Ever since their impromptu picnic he'd half-expected she might pull a runner. Which could still happen. The wide-eyed look she sent him as he helped her out of the vehicle while Robert got her bag from the trunk spoke volumes. He wondered if she had the faintest idea just how expressive her face could be. Or the effect her voice had had on him from day one.

She straightened and looked around as if she had no idea where she was or how she got there. "You said you'd take care of the flight. I assumed you meant a commercial airline."

"This is faster and way more convenient."

She continued to look around, her brow wrinkled in an endearing way he didn't see a lot in Hollywood. "I don't see the pilot."

"You're looking at him."

"*You're* flying us there?"

"Thanks, Robert," he said, taking April's overnight bag before she could change her mind and bolt. "I got this."

Robert hesitated. "Miss?"

"I'll let you know my return schedule," she said finally.

"Very good."

She looked at his Piper Meridian, the love of his life. "Is this thing even safe?"

"I wouldn't take her up if she wasn't. You can trust me April." Winning her trust had become his number one goal. "I've done all my pre-flight checks and filed the flight plan. Next stop Bremerton. From there we'll grab a rental car and head to Blue Sky Island." He stared skyward. "Perfect day to be up in the clouds. Weather in Seattle is good, so let's hope the island lives up to its name."

He ushered her up the steps and into the plane's spacious interior, stowing her overnight bag next to his duffel. He gave her the tour with a sweep of his hand. "Charging ports. Mineral water. Snacks. All the comforts of home. I'll be in the cockpit if you need me."

Her fists were clenched. "It seems awfully small."

"Five passengers max. Perfect size."

"How long does the flight take?"

"About two and a half hours. Settle in and enjoy the view." He took a closer look. She appeared paler than normal. "You're not afraid of flying, are you? Or heights? Need a Gravol? Afraid I'm all out of Ativan." He smiled to let her know he was kidding, but his attempted humor seemed to go right over her head.

She gave her head a jerky shake, sat down in the nearest seat and fumbled with her seatbelt.

"You can take a nap if you want."

"I don't nap."

"You want to sit up front with me?"

That same jerky shake of her head.

He shoved his hands in his pockets, wishing he knew the right thing to say to put her at ease, but putting people at their ease was not something he'd had a lot of experience with.

THEY WERE ABOUT HALFWAY through the flight when he heard her behind him. Her color looked a little better. She grabbed the back of the seat next to him and settled in. He passed her a headset. "You want to take the controls?"

Her eyes widened, as if unsure if he was serious or not. Even he didn't know. It wasn't an offer he'd made to anyone before. "The Oregon coast," he said, waving a hand to encompass the stretch of land they were flying over. "A lot less people than California. Beautiful stretches of isolated beaches."

She nodded.

"You been to the Emerald City before?"

Another head shake.

"You're not very chatty today, are you?"

She moistened her lips with the tip of her tongue. "I guess not."

"You're not worried about the wedding and not knowing anyone, are you? The bride recently started her own PR business. I know that's not the same as what you do, but it's a similar field. Now that I think of it, I heard Blaze pretended to be her fake boyfriend for a weekend so she could save face with some guy who dumped her when he showed up with his new squeeze."

"And now they're getting married. Am I supposed to find comfort in that?"

He laughed out loud. "This fake dating stuff was your idea not mine. Feel free to break up with me anytime you want."

Baxter snuck a sideways glance at her, thoroughly enjoying himself. For once he didn't have to worry about the day after a date, or the woman getting the wrong idea and him trying to let her down easy. Which was not exactly his forte. Letting them down easy. He didn't set out to break hearts; he was always upfront right from the start that he wasn't the settling down type. For some reason most women couldn't seem to resist that challenge, and went out of their way to make him change his mind. His standoffishness proved to be a bigger chick magnet than if he walked around with an engagement ring in his pocket.

He was actually happy to have April with him this weekend. In his experience, weddings tended to fire up the emotional needs of every single female within a two-block radius.

"It's certainly green," she said, leaning forward to view the land below.

"Hence the Emerald City."

"Oh." Silence. Then, "I didn't know there were so many islands off the coast. Do you know which one we're headed for?"

"I'm not sure." He pointed. "That's Mount Rainier over there. Further North, you can just see the peak of Mount Baker."

April's gaze shifted. "Mount Rainier looks beautiful."

He nodded. "I haven't flown up this way for a while. I forget how pretty the landscape is."

"Do you find it hard to take a commercial flight?"

"What do you mean?"

"Trusting the navigation to someone else."

"I haven't had occasion to since I got my license, but I have a feeling I wouldn't enjoy it much. The crowds if nothing else. And you're right about the control. You and I are both more comfortable when we're calling the shots."

"Which creates somewhat of a tug-of-war."

He extended a closed fist her way for a fist-bump. "May the best control freak win."

"I'll amend that to say, may we both get what we want."

Yup. He smiled to himself. No way was she giving him the last word.

Before long he spotted Bremerton up ahead and alerted the tower of their approach. Ten minutes later he set the Piper down gently and taxied to a stop in the spot he was directed to, shutting things down before he took off his headset and turned to face her. "That wasn't so bad now, was it?"

"I have a feeling I'm going to enjoy not taking half an hour to deplane."

"Or wait for luggage." Minutes later he stood as the stairs were wheeled up to the door and a taxi rolled up. He glanced at his watch. "Right on time. We'll grab the rental car and head to the island. There's a ferry that all the tourists take, hoping to see whales or other marine life, but the locals mainly use the bridge."

CHAPTER 7

B axter had it all wrong. She wasn't a control freak. An independent woman who knew her own mind, yes. Control freak no. A point she felt she proved very well by sitting quietly as Baxter made the arrangements with the rental company for the Jeep he'd ordered and plugged the island destination into his phone's GPS.

"What time is the wedding?"

"Three o'clock."

"And you're sure it's casual attire?"

"It's on the beach. Blaze told me it's flip flops all the way. What's wrong? You worried about not fitting in?"

April stifled a snort. Little did he know she'd never fit in anyplace her entire life, bounced from her mom's family to her dad's, never truly part of either, but she wasn't about to share that with him. "Men don't understand. It's a girl thing when it comes to what to wear to a wedding." She didn't have a lot of clothes that didn't scream 'work', but at the last minute had unearthed a simple, summer sundress that she'd forgotten about in the back of her closet, and hoped it wasn't too casual. She had a light shawl to throw over her shoulders when the temperature cooled off.

Since it was a celebrity wedding, she expected a slew of candid shots would wind up on social and it was important she present the right image.

After all, her entire life was about presenting the right image. She glanced sideways at Baxter. Other than having his sights set on this show, did he really not care what others thought of him?

She barely noticed when the road they were on turned into a bridge leading to the island. His phone chirped and he gave it a quick glance. "Good our rooms are ready."

She was relieved to hear him say 'rooms'. Not that she expected Baxter was the type to pull the old 'sorry but we have to share the last room on the island' stunt. From all accounts, women in his life were both plentiful and disposable.

The island appeared to have only one main road, which as far as she could tell closely followed the shoreline. They drove past a grade school, a marina, and a block-long collection of shops with a gallery, a coffee shop and a pharmacy.

"Not much here, is there?"

"I gather that's the charm of the place. Apparently, cruise ships flock here ever since they built a dock big enough." He glanced at his phone. "Not far now to the resort."

Siri directed them to Sunset Lodge, the sunset-colored name freshly painted on a sign made from a length-wise cut half-log atop two log pillars on either side of a gravel driveway. The tree-lined driveway took several leisurely twists and turns and the Jeep lurched over more than one pothole before they reached what looked like the main lodge perched atop a cliff overlooking the Pacific, and Siri assured them they had reached their destination. The wood-sided building greeted them with wide stairs that led to a huge, wrap-around porch overlooking the ocean. Even in the parking lot she could hear the roar of the waves. Baxter started toward the lodge.

"Don't we need our bags?"

"The lodge was full when I booked. We're bunking in one of the nearby cabins."

April stiffened. A cabin implied isolation. Intimacy.

"Don't worry. They all have running water and electricity. Except of course when the power goes out."

April wrapped her arms around herself. Towering cedars and firs reached for the skyline, unmoving in the stillness. Today was sunny and bright. But in the dead of winter the place would be dark and dismal, the trees groaning and creaking in the wind. She knew west coast storm-watching was a thing, but it wasn't an activity she was eager to embrace. She gave herself a mental shake. They were only here for one night.

"Coming?" Baxter held open one of the oversize wood and glass doors leading into the lodge.

His boot heels echoed on the shiny wood floor as she followed him to the front desk. No one was around, but she could smell the delicious scents of baking somewhere in the back. A huge great room facing the ocean stretched empty before them with a massive stone fireplace rimmed by couches and easy chairs. Baxter rang the bell. A minute later a middle-aged woman came into view, wiping her hands on her apron. She smiled in welcome. "The Reid party. Glad you made it. We'd almost given up."

Baxter signed in and passed over his credit card. The woman waved it away. "We'll square up when you leave." She pulled out a paper map of the property and drew a bright red line down what April assumed was the road, winding through the trees. "Go right at the next fork. Your cabin's on the left." She made an arrow with a circle around what April assumed was their cabin.

"Where are all the other guests?" April asked. She'd expected the lodge to be a hive of pre-wedding activity.

"Most of them are down at the beach already. It's a bit of a hike so we've got golf carts standing by to take you down when you're ready. You'll find a light snack in your cabin to tide you over before the wedding feast. Is there anything else?"

"Just the keys," Baxter said.

The woman, whose nametag read Millie, laughed. "No keys. There's a bolt on the inside of your door, but that's it. We trust our guests."

April's jaw dropped. No keys? She'd never heard of such a thing.

"I hope there's a safe in the cabin," April muttered as she followed Baxter back to the Jeep.

He shrugged. "Anything you want secured, I'll lock it in the Jeep for you." He handed her the map. "I'll leave you to navigate."

She settled back into her seat and smoothed the map to orient herself. "Look. The cabins must be all named after other nearby islands." Next to Moresby, there was a big red ring drawn around Orcas. "I hope we can hear the ocean from our rooms."

Orcas was a short distance from the other cabins, its deck out back facing the ocean and boasting a private hot tub. Inside the main room, floor-to-ceiling windows rose on either side of a wood-burning stove, while a tiny kitchenette with a coffee maker and a bar fridge was tucked against one wall. A doorway on either side of the room led to what April assumed were the two bedrooms. No television in sight.

"Which room would you like?"

"I don't mind."

Baxter poked his head into one, then crossed the room and did the same on the other side. "They're both the same." He glanced at his watch. "There's lots of time if you want to catch a shower or have a snack before you get changed. It's not quite two."

"Feel free join the others if you want," she said. "I'll meet you down there in a little while."

"I think I'd rather hang out here and soak up the atmosphere."

April cocked a brow. "If anything, I expected you to say you'd be getting some work done first."

"I promised myself a weekend with no work. Other than project 'make Baxter a media darling', and that's your department."

"It would be easier if I knew what to expect. Who will be here?"

"I guess we find all that out together."

"Are you and groom good friends?"

"We've done a number of films together."

"That's not what I asked."

"Define good friends."

April blew out a breath. She was one to talk. She'd given Baxter a hard time about not having anyone in his life, yet she wasn't much different. He might have moved constantly as a kid, but she had too. Shuttled from house to house like an unwanted relative who'd outstayed their welcome. The members of each household had a lifetime of shared experiences that she never seemed to quite be part of.

"Will you know most of the guests?"

"Most of the film people by sight, I expect. I don't have a clue who'll be here from the bride's side."

"Does the groom have family?"

Baxter crossed the room as if restless. "I guess we'll find out."

"What's the matter?"

He spun to face her. "To tell you the truth, I don't even know why I'm here. Blaze and I did a bunch of films together before his accident, but I've hardly seen him since. The one thing we had in common was that we were both unattached. Don't get me wrong. I'm happy for him and Kaitlyn. He was kind of a mess after the accident, and from what I've heard she's been really good for him. Lots of compromise on both their parts to make things work."

"Isn't compromise part of every relationship?"

"Yeah, but with his career based in LA and hers here—" Baxter ran a hand through his hair as if perplexed by the entire concept. "I suppose that might all change after the wedding, but the bride's family has lived on the island for generations."

April forced a smile. "Sounds to me like it should be a most interesting time ahead. I'd better go get ready."

In her room, April unpacked her toiletries and gave her dress a shake. Luckily, it was wrinkle-proof. The ensuite bathroom was functional and basic although the lighting left a little to be desired. Maybe no one wore make up here in the back of beyond. She went to check her email and quickly learned there was spotty cell reception and no wifi. Which made her phone's only purpose here a camera. She'd meant to post that cute humming bird picture before they left. Too bad she'd forgotten.

She gave herself a critical once over in the mirror on the back of the door. She'd forgotten how flattering this dress was, the full skirt flaring just below her knees while the fitted bodice made the most of her shape. The color was also complimentary. Bright summer splashes of fuchsia, yellow and turquoise were mixed in with other jewel tones and the waist was cinched with a wide purple belt. She added a touch more mascara and lipstick, tossed on a gossamer purple shawl and slid her feet into jewel-crusted flip-flops. Ready as she'd ever be.

Baxter turned when he heard her door open, and she was gratified to see his brow raise and his eyes widen in approval. He was wearing what one could easily call 'dress jeans' topped with a short-sleeved front button shirt in tropical colors with a parrot on the back.

"Look at us," he said. "We clean up good!"

"You smell good, too." Or was that the woods around them backgrounded by the salty surf? Nope something spicy and very, very masculine. "Let's go out on the deck and take a selfie with the ocean behind."

"A selfie! What for?"

"To show the world what a wonderful time we're having together." At least she would once she was back to civilization with wifi.

Baxter actually looked endearingly awkward, his back against the rail as she moved in next to him. Did he flinch when she brushed against him? She passed him the phone. "Your arms are longer. You hold it. Up high so we get a good sweep of water behind us." Her finger hovered near the camera button. "I'll take the picture."

He frowned. "I don't do selfies."

She smiled and tucked her head against his chest. "Put your other arm around me and smile. Pretend you're having a good time."

"How about this?" He leered.

"Stop it!" She elbowed him lightly in the ribs and he recoiled. She turned to him with a mischievous grin. "Don't tell me you're ticklish!" Her free hand probed his side as he tried to dodge her touch.

"Stop that!"

Which is when she pushed the button and got the perfect shot. To any outsider, they looked inseparable, both laughing as if they found total joy in each other's company. "Money shot!" She turned off the camera and tucked the phone into a tiny pink shoulder bag barely big enough for her phone, her lipstick and a tissue. As comfortably as if she'd been doing it all her life, she grabbed his wrist and checked his watch. "We should go."

They followed the gravel driveway back to the lodge where a young man was lounging behind the wheel of a golf cart. He jumped to his feet when he saw them. "Ready to go down?"

"Are we last?" Baxter helped April in then slid in next to her. He seemed unaware that his closest arm rested across the seat back and grazed her shoulder. She felt the warmth of his touch as he fingered the soft fabric of her shawl.

"Still waiting on the bride and her attendants." The cart jolted over the scrubby grass toward a narrow pathway where a series of switchbacks wound their way down the face of the cliff to a stunning, secluded sandy beach below. Two tidy sections of rows of white chairs, some already occupied, faced the ocean, divided by a stretch of blue carpet. To their far left, a grouping of event tents topped long, linen-covered banquet tables. Beyond that a plume of smoke rose not far from a massive metal barbeque.

"What a set up!" April said as the golf cart jerked to a stop a short distance from the chairs. More than a dozen Tiki torches were pushed into the sand near the tents. Guests congregated in small clusters, many of them near what April assumed was a portable bar.

She looked at their driver. "This must take some doing to get all set up."

The young man shrugged. "The resort only does events. After all these years, the owners have things down to a fine art."

April's stomach made an unladylike noise, reminding her she'd bypassed the snacks in their cabin. "Something smells delicious."

"Chef has a pig on the spit. Island raised. The pit has salmon baking. They'll be doing corn and fresh crab on the barbeque."

April smiled up at Baxter, pretending to smooth the collar of his shirt. "You hear that, Honey? All your favorites."

As the golf cart pulled a U-turn and headed back up the switchbacks, April looked up at Baxter. "Where to first?"

Before he could answer, three women descended as if they'd been watching for them. "Baxter," said the tallest one, whose hair was an enviable shade of thick, red-gold curls.

"Vivica," he said. "Tiff. Ramona. You ladies all look lovely."

"We wondered if you'd show your face."

April shifted from foot to foot, waiting for Baxter to make introductions. The other two, one blonde, one dark-haired, flanked their friend before, in a move that April could only consider rehearsed, Vivica stepped forward and delivered Baxter a resounding slap across the face.

"That's from us. Consider it your due."

April stood frozen while Baxter raised a hand to his jaw.

"Anyone else care for a swing?"

Vivica gave her head a shake that sent her curls bouncing down her back. "We drew straws. I got lucky." With that she turned on her heel. As her friends followed,

April realized they'd both been videotaping the incident. Wait till that hit social!

She tucked her arm through his in a protective gesture. "Are you okay?"

He ran a hand along his jaw as if making sure nothing was broken. "I'm fine."

"That'll make interesting viewing on someone's feed. Any other women scorned here tonight that you recognize?"

Baxter shrugged and took her arm. "I think I need a drink. Then I'll introduce you to Blaze before the ceremony starts."

Blaze, the groom, was handsome in a rugged sort of way, with a devil-may-care swagger that April assumed was his calling card. He introduced them both to his best man, Steve, adding that Steve was the bride's brother. "He didn't believe I was good enough for his little sis," Blaze said.

"Still don't," Steve kidded with a fake punch to Blaze's arms. "But I got overruled."

"What a great spot for a wedding," April said.

"You two should spend an hour exploring the island tomorrow before you leave," Steve said. "I'll give you a few tips later on things you need to see."

While Baxter talked shop with a few Hollywood types, April scanned the crowd. It was easy to pick out the LA guests from the locals, almost as if there was a visible divide. Hopefully, as the day wore on, people would loosen up and mingle, even if they did come from two different worlds.

Before long, the lovely melodic music of a harp sent everyone scrambling to find seats. Near the water, under a flower-decked arbor, Blaze and Steve waited next to a woman whom April assumed was the officiant. Everyone's heads craned at the sound of a golf cart approaching. Two women alighted. The first, the bride, was in a flowing calf-length dress, her auburn hair falling simply to her shoulders and wound through with wild flowers that matched her bouquet. Her attendant wore a short seafoam green dress. Both women smiled and took their places at the edge of the carpet. Someone, an event planner maybe, gave them a signal to start the procession.

"It's magical," April whispered to Baxter as the ceremony proceeded, the couple solemn-faced as they repeated their vows and exchanged rings. Everyone laughed when Blaze dropped the ring intended for Kaitlin and had to scrabble through the sand for it. The guests clapped and whistled as the couple exchanged their first married kiss before they moved over to sign the register.

Baxter shot her a cynical look. "You women always say that about a wedding."

April narrowed her gaze. "We *women*?"

She was saved from more Baxter-cynicism by the arrival of a man he knew who dragged him off a short distance for a low-voiced huddle.

He came back with kind of a bemused grin.

"Something you'd care to share?"

"Maybe later," he said.

Before long, wait staff moved through the crowd with trays of champagne for the guests and Baxter plucked two. His fingers brushed hers as he handed her the glass and rested his free arm loosely around her waist.

April flinched, then told herself to get used to it. People needed to believe they were a couple. Anything to refute that wretched face-slap video. She could just see the incident going viral and undoing everything they'd accomplished so far.

The murmur of voices died down as Blaze and Kaitlyn, hands linked between them, joined their guests.

Steve stepped forward. "Ladies and gentlemen, I give you Mr. and Mrs. Mahoney. He raised his glass. "To the bride and groom."

The toast rippled through the crowd. When she looked toward Baxter his eyes were firmly focused on her over the rim of his glass. His low voice was for her ears alone. "To us. I'm really glad you're here."

Sincerity rang through his tone and April didn't know how to respond. To say it was her job wasn't the appropriate response. Instead, she took a sip and glanced around. "What happens now?"

"I understand they have a spot picked out down the beach for the wedding photos. See that outcropping?"

April followed his gaze to where a random cluster of black rocks jettied from the smooth gray expanse of wet sand. A few people were already headed in that direction.

"I'll meet you over there in a few. There's something I need to do first."

"Try not to get into any more altercations with the 'ghosts of girlfriends past'," she said, quoting a movie title from years ago that seemed to fit.

"No one's earned girlfriend status in a long time," he said meaningfully. "I'm still trying to get a handle on my role this weekend."

She placed her glass on the tray of a passing server and kicked off her flip flops. Bending to pick them up, she heard her name and turned in surprise. An attractive brunette was waving and smiling.

"April, I'm Iris, Steve's girlfriend. He asked me to keep an eye out for you in case Baxter abandons you."

April laughed. "It seems he's been known for that."

"I wouldn't take anything you hear today seriously."

"What's the expression? Believe half of what you see and

none of what you hear." The two of them fell behind the slow exodus down the beach. "Did Steve abandon you, too?"

"He's up ahead with the wedding party."

"Wait up, sis!"

April turned when Iris did. A young woman ran toward them, shoes in hand. Iris did the introduction when she reached them. "Frannie, April. April, my little sister, Frannie."

"Sister?" The two women looked nothing alike, for Frannie was short with a head of riotous dark curls, a round face and freckles.

Iris shrugged. "Same mother, same father. Go figure."

Not a remark April could ever parrot. "I don't resemble any of my siblings either."

Frannie gave her a sizing-up look. "You're here with hunky Baxter Reid, the director. Good for you. Ignore what those bitter beotches say. They're just jealous they couldn't snag him."

April flushed. How many people here had witnessed the slap?

"Frannie. We were just saying how destructive gossip can be."

"It's not gossip. I heard them before you showed up, wondering who had gotten her claws into Baxter. Saying the poor thing would be sorry soon enough."

April pulled her sweetest media smile. "It seems poor Baxter has been misunderstood. He's very different from the guy the media presents. Do you both live here on the island?"

"Heavens, no," Iris said. "I'd go mad."

"Me, too," Frannie said. "I think you have to be born here to put up with it as your fulltime residence."

Before long they reached the picturesque grouping of

rocks that looked as if they'd been hewn by a sculptor's hand rather than Mother Nature. The bride and groom were posed with the sun behind them throwing the pair into silhouette. Totally frame-worthy, the image would make a wonderful memory.

As she smiled at the scene and the photographer moved around the couple adjusting her camera, two large canoes pulled into sight near shore, steered by a group of men in Viking gear, attacking each other with bows and arrows. Standing at the helm of one was Baxter.

CHAPTER 8

"What was that about?" April asked Baxter when he joined her a short time later.

He smirked. "Apparently Blaze is known for photo bombing his buddies' wedding photos with a goofy stunt, so a group of the guys decided it was payback time."

Even he had been amazed when he'd been pulled aside to be included. It turned out one of Blaze's stunt students had the costumes and props shipped out from a prop department to the resort last week and early this morning they'd been tucked away out of sight close to shore.

"And you felt compelled to join their ranks? In something so juvenile?"

He bit his lip to keep from laughing out loud. She looked so affronted. "It's all in fun, April. Weren't you telling me I take life too seriously?"

She gave a haughty lift to her chin. "I said no such thing."

"Well, someone did recently."

They stood in companionable silence as the bride and groom struck a variety of different poses on the rocks.

Around them, Baxter sensed people growing restless with some heading back to the main wedding area, but he was content to hang around next to April.

The realization shocked him. When was the last time he'd been content hanging around doing nothing, just being in the moment?

Never before meeting April.

He even felt different today. He felt a part of things, a participant instead of an observer. He'd spent his adult years viewing life from a safe distance behind the lens of a movie camera. Not needing to get involved.

Yet earlier, out in the canoe with the other guys it had felt good to be involved. To be part of something he'd remember for years. Writing his own story instead of directing someone else's.

He slid a sideways look toward April. He couldn't help but think that she was at least partly responsible for this shift he was feeling. Looking back, he could see the way he'd spent his youth building a protective wall around himself, not letting anyone close, a habit that had carried over into his adult life. People respected him from a distance but they never got to know the real him because he didn't let them in.

Some might even admire his ability to dodge life's bullets unscathed and come out ahead. But he'd missed a lot along the way. He'd certainly not endeared himself to anyone. Or shown the world that he was human. Somehow, April brought out his human side. The part of him that bled when he got hurt. The part he'd taken pains to suppress.

Looking up, he realized most of the guests had already drifted back. The bride and groom were off to one side in a huddle with the photographer.

"Looks like we should head back."

She nodded. Hard to tell what she was thinking. Not too long ago he wouldn't have cared. That realization shocked him! He'd not considered himself an uncaring person, but apparently he had been pretty self-absorbed.

April glanced over her shoulder and sighed. "The sun will be going down soon. They'll be able to get some awesome sunset shots."

He looked toward the West, wondering when was the last time he'd noticed the sun set, let alone watched it with a woman.

The tent beckoned, hundreds of mini lights twining up the columns holding up the canvas top. The tiki lights glowed against the sky. He could smell roast pork and grilling corn, this entire day a total departure from the stuffy church weddings favored by a lot of couples he'd seen take the plunge. Tables stretched beneath the canvas roof, most of the chairs already occupied.

"We'd better find seats. Where do you want to sit?"

Like him, she must have realized their choices were slim. "Depends if you can make nice."

He followed her gaze. "You seriously think we ought to join *The Three Witches of Eastwick* and their dates?"

"No time like the present to let the world know you're a changed man."

He linked his fingers through hers. "Promise you'll defend me if one of them comes at me with a dinner knife."

The comical look on the women's faces was worth it when he approached their table, pulled out the two empty chairs, and said, "Mind if we join you?" helping April into the closest chair before anyone could respond. The men eyed him with a mixture of surprise and respect while the women stared down at their plates.

"Baxter Reid," he said by way of introduction and

planted himself in the other chair. Just his luck he was across from Viv and whatever poor sod she was with. "My girlfriend, April Thomas." He was surprised how easily the girlfriend part slid off his tongue. "These lovely ladies I already know from the industry."

The men each introduced themselves, but their names went in one ear and out the other.

"You were part of the Viking crew earlier. That was a great 'gotcha' at Blaze."

"Not sure his new wife will feel that way when she looks at the wedding photos," Baxter said. "You guys friends of Blaze or Kaitlyn?"

It turned out all three men were from LA, friends of Blaze.

"How about you?" Viv's guy asked.

"I directed a number of films he was in."

"That's why your name is familiar. I really enjoyed your last film," piped up the guy on his side of the table, next to April. "What are you working on these days?"

"We just wrapped the latest Holly Snow film, *Wicked Ways*. Do you gents work in the industry?"

"Not a chance," Tiff's date said.

"No way," said the first guy.

As if on cue, business cards were produced. A real estate agent, a stockbroker, and a computer analyst. Baxter tucked them carefully in his wallet.

"White or red, sir?" asked a server at his elbow holding two bottles of wine.

"Red for me, please. White for the lady." He hoped April liked white wine. It felt like the safer bet.

Dusk began to settle in, candlelight on the tables throwing a romantic glow over the table. Baxter caught himself. Since when did he consider candlelight romantic? Unless it was mentioned in a script.

"So, April, tell us how you two met?" Viv asked. She'd always been loud and nosy and the years hadn't mellowed her any. Not even the candlelight could soften her sharp features and hungry look. She'd glommed onto him as a way to instant stardom but he was nobody's fool and didn't suffer her company for long.

He saw a stab of panic in April's eyes as they flew to meet his. They hadn't really collaborated on a story and he was curious to hear what she'd say.

"We met through my brother, Christopher," she said, finally. He noticed her pleating the napkin with her fingers. She'd done that on their picnic as well. Must be a nervous habit. "Chris sells cars and you know boys and their toys." She forced a nervous laugh, and he stepped in.

"In the end I never did buy a car off Chris, although I might have had I known it would get me an introduction to this lady." He put his arm around her shoulders and gave an affectionate squeeze. She felt cold. "Chris and my agent Mike are good friends. About a week later I was playing in a fundraising softball tournament. I hit one into the stands, and guess who caught it? I recognized Chris and Mike with April sitting between them holding my ball in both hands." He gave a lecherous chuckle. "Could have been my heart. I made a point after the game to make sure I got an introduction." He gave a deprecating shrug. "A lady in LA can't be too careful who she meets up with, but I trusted the guys she was with would vouch that I was nothing like my reputation might suggest."

April, who had visibly relaxed as he spoke, now piped in the way he had hoped she would. "At first, I turned him down.

I'd heard some of those director's couch stories," she smiled around the table. "But he was persistent." She sent a dainty smile his way. "I believe everyone deserves a chance, despite the public's perception or media reports about them." She paused for breath. All eyes at the table were on her expectantly. "Our first date was a total surprise. Chris must have told Baxter how much I love Laguna Beach, so that's where he took me. We were inside my favorite gallery, and he insisted on buying me this adorable humming bird. Look. Isn't it cute?" She pulled out her phone. He raised his brow when he saw the hummingbird as her screensaver. She passed the phone around.

Viv grabbed it first, gave it a cursory glance then passed it on. "Baxter Reid in an art gallery. Who could have imagined? He took me to a boxing match."

Which was true. He'd been trying to show her he wasn't her type and let her down easy, but it hadn't worked.

Tiff and Ramona were watching him with identical cynical looks. He didn't remember any specific date with either of them, and hoped no one quizzed him on it.

"Another time he surprised me with a picnic at Barnsdall Art Park."

Tiff tried and failed to raise a Botoxed brow. "Baxter planned a picnic?"

April laughed. "I wouldn't go that far. I expect the deli gets the actual credit, but the food he chose was out of this world."

"Hmmph." Tiff stared at an inch-long fingernail as if she was looking at her reflection.

Baxter was relieved when Tom the realtor broke in. He raised his wine glass. "I say we toast the bride and groom for inviting us to this fabulous hidden gem of a resort for this memorable evening. Baxter, April, it's a pleasure to meet you both."

Shortly after that, the head table speeches took everyone's attention, followed by the meal and cake cutting before a group of musicians took over the instruments on a makeshift stage wedged in one corner.

Baxter sat back, contentment rippling through him as the bride and groom danced their first dance together. Pretty soon other guests joined in, inside the tent and out on the beach where dry sand flew through the air, stirred up by the dancers.

"Hear that, darling? They're playing our song." Baxter turned to April, rose and held a hand her way.

"I didn't know we had a song," she murmured as he pulled her into his arms.

"We do now. Especially since I've had enough of our dining companions."

April threw back her head and laughed. "Not used to being a bug under a microscope?"

"Not with Viv there ready to pick my wings off."

His hand on the small of her back nudged her a bit closer. "I must say, though, I think we passed with flying colors."

She tilted her head toward his. "Yeah? You think they bought that we're a couple?"

Where did the sudden urge to lean down and kiss her come from?

"How long do you think we need to hang around?"

"It would be rude to leave before the bride and groom do."

"Right."

He glared over at Blaze. Hurry up and leave man. Don't you want to be alone with your blushing bride? Because he sure as heck wanted to be alone with April. Away from everyone watching them, judging their every move.

After a while the band took a break, which left them little choice but to return to their seats. Tom reached across the table and passed something to Baxter. His license.

"Spotted this under your chair. It must have fallen out of your wallet."

"Thanks." As he went to put it away, he noticed Viv smirking across the table at him. He gave her a hard stare.

Viv turned to Tom. "Tell Ernest he's welcome, Tom."

Right! They would have seen his full name.

"I can't for the life of me think why you would use your middle name," Viv said with mock sweetness. Tom gave a sympathetic lift of his brow.

Baxter gritted his teeth. He couldn't let Viv see she was getting to him. "Baxter is my mother's maiden name. I use it as a tribute to her." He almost said to her memory, but that wasn't right when the poor thing was still alive, if you could call it that.

"You even look like an Ernest," Viv said, continuing to bait him.

He felt April next to him, her fingers digging into his thigh in support, and instantly relaxed. It felt nice to have an ally.

"Captain Ernest Reid is my old man," Baxter said calmy. "I'm nothing like him, so never saw any point in using his name." He picked up the wine bottle in the middle of the table and poured himself a healthy splash. "Far as I could tell, he was relieved. He always thought Hollywood was for sissies. He's never met guys like Blaze who put their life on the line every day."

The musicians ran back on stage and took up their instruments, the drummer gave the crowd a drumroll and Steve led the applause for the newlyweds who came forward in matching motorcycle leathers. Baxter grinned. A nontraditional wedding scene all the way. The bride and groom gave the guests a wave as the band played 'White Wedding'. Moments later, the roar of Blaze's Harley drowned out the music for a short time. As the lead singer encouraged everyone to stay and enjoy the music, Baxter turned to April.

"Shall we?"

"Of course." She rose. "Good night, everyone. Lovely to meet you all."

A murmur of good nights ran around the table. The last parting remark came from Viv, punctuated with a waggle of her fingers. "Bye, April. Bye Ernest."

Staff members were at the ready next to a line of waiting golfcarts and Baxter leapt into the first one he saw, pulling April with him.

As their driver started up the switchback, Baxter turned to her. "Did I mention my dislike, generally, of weddings?"

"I don't know," she said. "I thought this one was pretty fun in its uniqueness, and I love the setting. Personally, I appreciated being spared the archaic custom of the single women fighting to see who catches the bride's bouquet."

"Ditto the garter," he said. Over the years he had amassed quite a collection. "Steve texted me a few suggestions of places on the island we should check out tomorrow before we leave. You game?"

He sensed her hesitation and suddenly it felt important to spend another day in her company. "Come on," he said. "We're here on this island getaway. When's the last time you took an entire weekend off?"

"All right. On one condition."

"What's that?"

"I know Viv hit a nerve with the Ernest bit. I think we need to spin it somehow. Make you out to be Earnest Ernest.

Well-meaning, sincere, nothing like the way you've been painted in the past."

He narrowed his gaze. "I'm not suddenly having people call me Ernest."

"That's not what I was thinking. But there has to be a way we can use it to your advantage."

CHAPTER 9

April woke up the next morning and out of habit, reached for her phone to check her email, before she flopped back onto her pillow and smoothed a hand through her bedhead hair. Right. No wifi. No email. And a reluctant promise to spend today sightseeing with Baxter before they left.

"You could have said no," she told herself as she rose and pushed the curtains open, surprised to see the morning sky was an ominous gray, while whitecaps dotted the angry waves heading for shore. What a difference from yesterday.

She pulled on her robe and opened the door. In the main room of the cabin, Baxter was already dressed and at the table drinking coffee. "They left coffee and muffins at the door," he said when she appeared. "Or there's a hot breakfast up at the lodge if you're hungry."

She shook her head and helped herself to a pottery mug from the shelf above the sink which she filled from the insulated carafe on the counter. "I'm still full from last night's feast." She waved a hand toward the window. "What happened to yesterday's blue sky?"

"Typical Pacific Northwest."

"Will it affect our trip back?"

"No. This was forecast when I checked the weather yesterday when we landed. It's supposed to blow over by the afternoon."

He glanced her way and April instinctively tightened the belt on her robe. Not that she felt unsafe around Baxter. Quite the contrary. He'd noticeably mellowed since their first meeting. She' might even go so far as to say she'd found his company enjoyable yesterday. A lot of guys wouldn't have taken the face slap in stride and managed to be sociable with the same group later. She was pretty sure that turning the other cheek was a big deal for him.

His gaze on her was heavy-lidded. "You sleep okay?"

"Out like a light," she said. "You?"

"It's a little too quiet here for my taste."

"I never heard a sound from the wedding after we got back. I wonder how long before everyone left?"

"I heard a few car doors slam around eleven thirty, but that was it."

She suddenly felt self-conscious. This setting was far too intimate, like a real couple away for the weekend and planning their day. "I'll just shower and get packed up."

"Take your time. I'll go square up with the office."

She gave him a second searching look. Not the response she would have expected from the Baxter she met a few weeks earlier, or the man she'd dragged off to Laguna Beach. Totally out of character; him contentedly sitting here looking out the window.

Grateful she'd worn jeans yesterday, and a sweater, April quickly got ready to go. When she returned, Baxter was sitting right where she'd left him, obviously lost in thought. She cleared her throat twice before he looked up.

He straightened and stretched. "It's nice here. Relaxing." He got up, took one last look around before he grabbed his coat and their bags, closed the door behind them, and loaded their things into the back of the Jeep.

Once seated behind the wheel, he turned to her before he started the Jeep. "I want to thank you for being here with me."

Another unexpected move on his part. "You're welcome."

"It's nice to take a date to a wedding without her itching to launch into her own wedding plans."

"Clearly, you've been hanging out with the wrong kind of women."

"I realize that now."

His gaze held hers for a beat or two before he turned the ignition. "According to Steve, we turn right at the main road, drive away from town and follow the coast road away from civilization."

"This is their idea of civilization?'

"Sure. Tidy little town. Cruise ship dock. Marinas."

"A veritable hub of activity," she said drily.

"Last night you said you liked the wedding venue."

"That's because I was full of fresh crab. And it was cool, just the wedding guests on that secluded beach, all set up like something out of a fairy tale."

He smiled. "Complete with Viking warriors."

"That was quite the stunt you guys pulled off. Did you hear if the bride was upset about her photos?"

"Blaze said she took it in stride."

They drove for miles without passing another car. "I had no idea the island was so big, did you?"

"Lots of people call this home year-round. Steve said there are over forty secluded coves and beaches. Lots of hiking trails. Pretty soon we should see the place where the surfers hang out."

April looked out over the ocean. "Is it me, or is it getting stormier by the second?"

"You might be right. Keep checking your phone. There must be someplace on this island with a signal that we can get the updated weather forecast."

"Maybe we should turn around."

He raised a brow. "And miss visiting the old hippie commune where a few holdouts still live off the grid?"

"And the bride's brother considers that a point of interest?"

As they continued on their way, the sky grew noticeably darker while the sea churned, some waves splashing nearly as high as the road. April saw a few fat splats of rain land on the windshield and pulled her sweater closer against her.

Behind the wheel, Baxter appeared totally relaxed despite the way the road wound narrowly next to the ocean, hugging the intimidating rock cliffs on the other side. She could see how steeply the bank dropped off directly below them.

He must have sensed her unease. "What is it?"

"I think maybe we should turn around. We don't know for sure if we're headed the right way or drove right past wherever it is we're supposed to be headed."

"Tell you what. I'll turn around when you see a place that's safe to do so."

It wasn't like her to be a worry wart. But being carjacked had taught her to err on the side of caution, even as she reminded herself Baxter knew what he was doing. "You're the driver." She leaned forward and fiddled with the radio dial, but nothing came through except sporadic bursts of static and she soon gave up.

He reached across and rested one hand on her thigh. "Maybe this was a bad idea. I can see you're not exactly enjoying the sights."

"I'm not typically a Nervous Nellie, but there's something in the air, more than salt." Her joke fell flat.

"I'll turn around as soon as I can."

Unfortunately, a place to safely turn around on the narrow roadway didn't appear for several miles.

"This should do," Baxter said as he slowed the Jeep.

She was glad it was him behind the wheel. No way she would want to attempt a turn around so close to the drop off.

It was raining for real now, no pretense but a serious, steady downpour driven furiously their way by the wind that also whipped the waves into a frenzy. The windshield wipers squeaked against the glass, working high speed to keep the window clear. The rear window was totally fogged up, making visibility difficult as Baxter carefully backed the Jeep onto the shoulder. There was an abrupt jolt as the rear of the vehicle slid backwards leaving the Jeep resting at an awkward angle, but Baxter didn't flinch, just eased on the gas as he concentrated on maneuvering the vehicle back and forth, bit by bit, until they were turned around and faced the other way.

"That was close," April said, once they were headed back the way they came. "I was afraid we might get stuck."

"Looked like brush beside the road back there, but it must have been covering up a ditch. After a full day of rain, we could have been stuck."

April shivered. This whole experience was taking her back to the night of the carjacking, her feeling of powerlessness. But this wasn't then. And Baxter wasn't that maniac. As the Jeep ate up the miles back toward the island's hub, her fists unclenched as she started to relax.

"Still no signal?" Baxter asked.

She glanced at her phone's screen and shook her head.

Baxter glanced at his watch. "With luck we'll be at the airport in a couple of hours, more or less."

April nodded and continued to stare out the window. Firs and Cedars, tortured by the wind, some bent and twisted, crested the top of the rocky cliffs and climbed up the mountain slopes toward where faraway hilltops loomed barren and gray, shorn bald by logging activity.

"It's nice these trees were spared."

"Probably second growth," Baxter said. "Some of them are pretty skinny."

April nodded and tried the radio again. Nothing but static. Suddenly there was a loud crack. Branches scratched the side and rear of the Jeep as Baxter accelerated, tires spinning on the slick pavement. April looked over her shoulder and gasped. A tree lay across the road, right where they'd driven seconds earlier.

Baxter glanced in the rearview mirror. "Close one."

April nodded jerkily.

"With this wind, it's unlikely the ferry will be running. Probably why they built a bridge."

April took a breath and forced herself to think about the upcoming schedule of events she was working to organize, and not just for project Baxter, although his job seemed to be occupying all her time lately. It would be interesting to get back on line and see how the influencers were reacting to the subtle changes in Baxter's MO. And what the celebrity gossips thought about them as a couple.

She caught her thoughts. Obviously they weren't really a couple, even if that was the façade being presented right now. She made a mental note to contact Mike in the morning and see if he'd heard any more about the *Sentry* project. She'd thrown herself wholeheartedly into this Baxter situation without thinking it through to where they eventually went their separate ways.

"A dime for your thoughts," Baxter said.

She smiled. "A dime?"

"Inflation."

"Just thinking ahead to the best way to extricate ourselves from each other."

"You're already planning how to break up with me?" He managed to sound hurt.

"I know being the dumper is usually your role, but I don't think it would go over very well if you dumped me. It needs to be the other way around."

He pushed out his bottom lip. "Can't it be mutual?"

"You're suggesting a compromise so soon?"

"Hey! I'm nothing if not a quick study. A lot of what you said is true. Like it or not, I'm a product of my upbringing. I never wanted to be like my old man. But his beliefs are planted deep. Change won't happen overnight."

"All we can hope is that the powers-that-be have a short memory, and buy into Earnest-Ernest." She turned his way. "You never told me why you want this show so badly."

Baxter barked out a laugh. "That's the ironic part. Originally, I wanted it strictly for the glory. No other reason than I want to get my hands on that shiny Oscar trophy to snub my nose at any naysayers."

"And now?"

"Now I want to make the best darn film that I can. If only to give those kids in the hospital a temporary distraction from their situation. To catapult them into a different world where good triumphs over evil and the world makes sense.

I'm in a position where I can do some good. Nurture some unknown talent. Lend my efforts to a worthy cause."

April straightened. "Wow! You've convinced me. Keep this up and I'll be out of a job soon. You won't need your image polished to a glossy sheen."

He cracked a smile. "Oh, I'll still need you, April. If only to make sure I don't lapse back into my old ways."

"I'll leave you my twelve-step guide so you can self-monitor. Oh, look, we must be getting close. I can just make out a few boats at the marina off in the distance." Then it hit her. There were no lights anywhere, not even the sign advertising the Marina Pub.

"Power must be out," she said in a small voice.

Baxter nodded. "I figured that a while ago. It won't affect the bridge. And luckily we have lots of gas, so we're good." He shot her a look. "There's nothing to worry about."

"The entire island looks deserted."

"That's because people either left before the storm or they're hunkered in where it's dry. Don't worry. It won't be anything like when the power goes out in LA."

"You must think I'm a worry wart. I'm not really."

He gave an endearing half-smile. "The two faces of April. Calm, cool, controlled and in charge. Yet, every once in a while, I see a glimpse of this other person. Not so sure of herself or in control as she pretends. It's an interesting transition."

"Hmmph." April hated to think she was so transparent. She'd created her own, very precise persona long before she started working on images of others. She didn't like to think there might be cracks in the veneer.

All of a sudden Baxter slammed on the brakes.

"What?" She peered through the gloom to see the Jeep's

headlights illuminate a half-drowned sign in the middle of the road. *Bridge closed.*

"How can they close the bridge?"

"It could be precautionary." Baxter backed up and turned left to continue down the street toward town, but they hadn't gone two blocks before they came across a second sign. *Road closed.*

Beyond the sign, the Jeep's headlights shone on a torrent of water rushing across the road. Baxter blew out a breath. "I'm getting my practice turning around in tight spots today."

"What do we do now?"

"I propose we head back to the resort and sit this out."

"With no power or cell service?"

"You have a better idea, miss control freak? Maybe they have a satellite phone at the resort for use in emergencies."

April found the thought oddly comforting. Surely island residents weren't stranded and cut off from the outside world on a regular basis.

Her comfort dissipated when they approached the driveway to the resort, only to find their way blocked by a bright yellow iron gate across the driveway.

Now what? She sat dumbfounded, vaguely aware of Baxter reaching into the back seat for his coat and opening his door. He left the Jeep running, its headlights illuminating the gate as he veered toward a heavy-looking silver metal chain at one end. Was that a padlock attached to it?

What were the chances? Unexpected storm. Power failure. Bridge closed. Road washed out. Resort abandoned and locked up tight. It was like something out of a B movie.

A B movie where the hero always prevailed! For somehow Baxter had unlocked the gate and was walking it away from the Jeep, leaving enough room for them to drive through.

He got back behind the wheel and slammed the door, pausing to slick his wet hair back from his forehead. "Padlock was just for show. Probably acts as enough of a deterrent to outsiders while the staff can come and go as needed."

"I guess it makes sense to keep the way in blocked, since they don't lock the individual cabins."

After he closed the gate behind them, Baxter drove on and stopped at the lodge, which was predictably in darkness. April would have been heartened to see a plume of smoke rising out of the massive rock chimney soaring high above the roofline, but no such luck.

They ran up the wide steps to the front door. Locked. "So much for not locking the place up," Baxter said, shading his eyes with his to look inside.

"They're bound to have cellars of wine and freezers full of food," she said. "It would be foolish to leave it open."

"At least the cabin won't be locked." He started toward the Jeep.

"You mean, we should just stay here. Without checking with anyone?"

"I'm happy to check in if anyone shows up. In the meantime, I don't see much other choice."

After the short, jouncing ride to Orcas they parked out front and made a run for it. The cabin was neat as a pin, no evidence they'd been there the previous night. Coffee cups had been put away and a clean towel hung over the rod near the sink. She peered into the closest bedroom where the bed had been neatly made.

"Home sweet home." Baxter dropped their bags near the door.

April pulled her sweater closer, wishing she had warmer

clothing. Absently she rubbed her hands together to warm them.

He gave her a close look. "Why don't you grab a hot bath before the water gets cold while I light a fire?"

"You're wet, too."

He gave her a cocky grin. "Lucky the tub looks big enough for two."

She eyed him through narrowed lids. "I'll save you my water. Maybe."

His laughter followed her through the closed door between the bedroom and the bathroom. It looked to be a very long day and night.

THE FIRE WAS CRACKLING in the wood stove, and the chill was off the room by the time she'd finished her bath and joined Baxter in the main living area. She felt much more in control, carrying a file folder that contained the roughed-out schedule for the next few weeks that she'd had the foresight to print before she left.

"Bath water's still warm if you want it."

"Thanks, but I had a quick shower. Almost made it before the hot water ran out. I made you some tea and foraged for snacks. Luckily our welcome basket from yesterday was still in the mini fridge."

April remained stalled on the "I made you some tea" part of the conversation. His thoughtfulness, never mind the fact that he even knew she drank tea. "How'd you heat the water?"

He pointed to a saucepan on the woodstove. "The old-fashioned way. No milk though, sorry."

"That's okay." A fat Brown Betty teapot wearing a hand-knit woolen tea cozy stood on the counter next to the sink, alongside one of the pottery mugs, probably made by a local artist. "Do you want some?"

He shook his head and indicated a plate in the middle of the trunk that doubled as a coffee table, laid out with fruit, cheese, crackers, and cured meat, all clumsily arranged in a sort of semi-circle around a ramakin of olives and pickles.

She set down her file folder and fetched a cup of tea before she sat down cross-legged on the floor near the fire. "You're getting lots of practice at this picnic stuff. Do you ever cook for real?"

"Nah. Never saw the point."

"Hmmmm...."

"Hmmmm what? I don't like that scheming look I see."

"Nothing." Nothing besides what fun it would be to get him booked as a guest on a local cooking show. Give viewers a glimpse of a different side of him. She sipped her tea and reached for a wedge of cheese before she glanced out the window. The wind howled, lashing rain against the window-pane, almost as if to taunt her.

He pointed to the folder. "That looks like work. I thought we were here to relax."

"How do you expect me to relax when we are literally stranded on a deserted island in the middle of storm?"

"Aren't you exaggerating?"

"I feel like I'm an extra in *The Shining*," she said, naming a psychological thriller set in a deserted resort, cut off from the outside world during a snowstorm.

"You're not old enough to have seen that movie."

"Bets? One of my brothers put it on one night when he was babysitting us younger kids. He thought it was funny to scare the bejeebers out of us. Which kind of blew up in his face when we all refused to go to bed and ruined his plans to be alone with his girlfriend." Defiantly she opened the folder and pulled out several sheets of paper.

Baxter reached forward, struck a match and lit a white pillar candle in its holder which he pushed toward her. "Don't wreck your eyes."

April looked down. Another unexpectedly thoughtful gesture. Could she have misjudged him when they met? Was his arrogant brashness all a coverup? Or had his actions lately been contrived, letting her think her tactics were working and that he'd changed his ways.

"Some of these events are flexible, working around anything unforeseen that crops up with your work. But not this one." She pointed to an entry she'd highlighted in bright yellow.

He grabbed a pillow, stuck it behind his head and stretched out on the couch. Or tried to. The couch was more like a loveseat, his legs dangled over one end.

"What's the event?"

"You're giving a presentation to a high school film-making class."

He bolted upright. "For real?"

"And you're going to draw the name of one lucky student to join you on set for a day-in-the-life."

"Babysitting!"

"Think of it as public relations! That age group lives on their phones and the lucky winner will no doubt be posting his or her experiences all over social. In fact, gender biases aside, it would be better if the student was a female. Women directors have really had to struggle to get ahead in the industry."

Baxter blew out a breath. "Why do I get the feeling you're enjoying this just a little too much?"

She closed the file folder and rested her elbows on her

lap. "Just so you know, I hate to lose. Therefore, you will be the front runner for this film of your heart if it's the last thing I do."

He leaned forward, the candlelight casting intriguing shadows on his face. "I've never seen this side of you."

"Oh, it's there. Make no mistake. I will do whatever it takes for you to achieve what you're after."

"Even if it's not the film of my heart?"

She narrowed her gaze. "What do you mean?"

"What we talked about earlier. The reasons I wanted to direct films in the first place, and how I lost that focus in the feeding frenzy of bankable stars and opening week revenues."

"I think that happens with everything. Especially anything artistic." She cocked her head. "What originally drew you to a career in film?"

"The usual idealistic assumption that I could do a better job than a lot of the movies out there. I looked for scripts with substance, carrying a message, but in an entertaining way. I wanted to either change the world or give people an escape from the one they're in. Not sure which. Both I guess. I wanted to touch people's lives, to make a difference. Then I hooked up with Mike and it became a numbers game, a popularity contest, measurable success. Which meant making the Oscar run."

"You came close."

"Close only counts in horseshoes."

"I thought it was hand grenades."

"That, too. Anyway, winning that coveted gold statue might be one way to get what I want, but I've recently come to realize it's not necessarily the only way. Plus, there's something else."

"What's that?"

"I've come to realize that being driven to the extreme can ultimately lead to self-destruction. Heck, I've seen it happen with others. Just never thought the same malaise might apply to me."

"You figured all this out based on what's been happening around you lately?"

"What you've made happen lately."

April's breath caught in her throat. This weekend was going off in all the wrong directions. Baxter wasn't supposed to be like this. Kind, caring and thoughtful, with deep feelings he wasn't afraid to express. Like someone she could fall for.

She jumped up. "How about a game of crib? I saw a board and deck of cards in one of the drawers."

"Sure." She could feel him watching her from beneath heavy-lidded eyes, a thoughtful look on his face as if he knew exactly what she was doing. Bolting from a situation that made her uncomfortable.

CHAPTER 10

Baxter shuffled the worn deck of cards then pushed them toward April to cut before he dealt them each six cards and laid the pack face down. The snack plate was pretty much depleted. He'd been in and out several times to bring in more wood from a box on the porch, and stoke the fire as darkness fell outside.

He watched the way candlelight softened her features as she rearranged her cards, frowning as she decided which two to discard for the dealer's hand. It was weird the way he opened up around her, sharing things he might have thought in the wee hours but never said aloud.

He tossed a pair of fives into the crib, knowing there was a good chance April would unload at least one ten or face card.

It also hadn't escaped his notice when she changed the subject abruptly. He didn't get it. He thought women were supposed to like it when a guy opened up, laid his guts bare on the table. Not so with April. His gaze narrowed. Could be she didn't feel in control of the situation and that freaked her out.

Decision finalized, she added two cards to his pair and flipped over the top card of the deck. Sweet! Another five! So far April was in the lead, but his crib hand should be a beauty. She claimed she didn't like to lose. Maybe it was high time someone bested her.

They played through their hands, April pegging extra points every chance she got. As he suspected, she'd kept all lower cards to hit 'thirty-one for two.' He let her have that small victory. He had his eye on a bigger prize.

She counted first. Her hand was soft. Only six points, even with the common five. He tried not to gloat as he put down his hand and counted his double run, adding the fours and sixes to make fifteens with the five on top.

Then he flipped over his crib. Yup. A jack and a king from

April. Sixteen points and one for the Jack. He roared ahead to the finish, leaving her lagging behind the skunk line.

Her mouth tightened as she gathered up the cards. "Again!"

He shook his head. "Not this guy. I know enough to quit while I'm ahead. Besides, you won the first four games. Makes you the reigning champ."

Reluctantly she packed up the cards and the board, then rose to put them away. "Poor loser."

He jumped to his feet and stared her down. "Who are you calling a loser?" The room, not very big to start with, suddenly felt claustrophobic with him blocking her way.

"Get out of my way, Baxter."

"Gonna make me?"

It happened in the blink of an eye. Color leached from her face, her eyes grew wide with panic.

Damn it! He'd forgotten she'd been traumatized, maybe

even hurt by someone bigger and stronger than she was. What if he was the first man she'd been alone with since the incident? He might not understand women very well, but he knew fear when he smelled it.

"Sorry!" He rubbed a hand through his hair and stepped aside. "I didn't mean to make you feel hemmed in."

She nodded, eyes downcast as she stepped around him and put the game away. With distance once more between them, her color returned to normal as she faced him from across the room. "Just so you know, it's not you. It's—" She bit off her words as if searching for the right one.

"Hey, we all have our triggers. My old man was a brute and a bully. I'd hate for anyone to think I was cut from the same cloth."

She shook her head. "Neither of those things. Arrogant, for sure. Cocky in fact. And definitely demeaning toward people you feel are your inferiors. But not a bully."

"Don't sugar coat the way you feel."

"Never."

"So why'd you take me on if I'm all those things you despise?"

She smiled then. "I told you before, I hate to lose. The bigger the challenge, the sweeter the victory."

He tilted his head as he took a step closer. "So that's all I was. A challenge?"

"Maybe. Or maybe we have more in common than either of us realized. Maybe I hoped I could get you to see the error of your ways. Hire some women. Do your part toward making the industry less divisive."

He dropped his voice an octave. Intimacy crackled through the air between them. "How'm I doing so far?" Had he taken another step closer, or had she?

"You're showing potential."

He wanted to show more than just potential. He wanted — As his gaze wandered to the darkness outside, he froze.

She reacted immediately. Stepped closer to him. "What is it?"

"Outside. I saw a light moving through the trees."

She cast him a wide-eyed, deer-in-the-headlights look before their gazes simultaneously flew to the door, which he hadn't locked after bringing in the last load of wood. Instinctively he moved to place himself between her and the door. He placed a finger to his lips warning her to stay quiet. The light came closer, shining through the window and throwing shadows on the wall behind them. He felt her stiffen and reached toward her with a reassuring hand. She clasped his forearm tight for a minute, then let go.

They heard the stomp of heavy boots on the porch. Whoever it was, they were making no effort to be quiet. He was edging toward the door when there was a pounding of fist against wood. Two strides took Baxter to the door. He flung it open.

He could just make out the figure of a man holding a large flashlight which he shone directly at Baxter, swept it through the room behind him, then directed it away.

"No one's supposed to be here. The lodge is closed."

"We were here last night."

The man nodded. "At the wedding. I recognize you."

"We tried to leave earlier but the bridge was closed. We had no place else to go."

"Someone should be here in the morning. You need anything?"

Baxter shook his head. "Any idea how long the power will be out?"

"Could be days before a crew gets over here. I came to

fire up the generator to keep the fridges and freezers going. Saw the light."

Baxter shrugged. "They have my card on file. We weren't going to skip out without paying."

"Well, goodnight then. The storm has nearly blown itself out. Then the cleanup starts."

Baxter recalled the tree narrowly missing them as it landed across the road. "Hopefully we can head out first thing tomorrow."

The man gave a salute, turned and left.

Baxter locked the door and turned around to update April, but she was gone, the door to her bedroom firmly closed.

Without even saying goodnight.

Baxter stared at the door panel and wondered what she was running from.

WHAT A DIFFERENCE A DAY MAKES! Sunlight spilled through the bedroom window as if apologizing for yesterday's storm. She clicked the light switch. Still no power. Good thing the place wasn't on a well, she thought as she brushed her teeth, or they wouldn't have any water either. She was looking forward to getting home and having a hot shower, never mind connecting with the outside world.

Being isolated here with Baxter had been—different. Definitely outside of her comfort zone, even though he'd done his best to put her at ease. She zipped her bag closed and carried it through to the cabin's main room.

Steam was rising from a pot of water Baxter was tending on the wood stove. "Ever had camp coffee?"

She shook her head.

"It's where you dump ground coffee into a pot of boiling water, let it sit for a while and pour off the top of the brew."

"Like a French Press?"

"A poor man's version of the French press."

He stirred the saucepan, staring at its contents before he met her gaze. "You disappeared last night."

"I was just really tired all of a sudden. You seemed to have things under control and so—"

"Did that bother you? Abdicating control?"

"Don't be ridiculous, I told you I was just tired."

He abandoned the coffee and came toward her. The room suddenly shrank. There wasn't enough air.

"What's wrong? Afraid I might have tried to kiss you goodnight?"

"N—nothing like that." More like afraid she might want him to kiss her.

"I think I'm getting a pretty clear picture. Not only are you good at creating images for other people, somewhere along the way you fine-tuned one for yourself. Anytime it seems that image might start to slip, maybe even expose you for the fraud that you are, you retreat to safety. You felt safe sitting here beating me at cards. You didn't feel safe when you thought you might need my protection."

She stiffened, drew herself to her full height. "I don't need your protection."

"I know you don't. But it shouldn't be scary to know it's there if you ever do need it."

Which in itself, was the scariest thing of all. But there was no way to explain that.

He turned back to the coffee. "Want to try my coffee mud?"

"No thank you. I'd like to get back as soon as possible."

He took a few sips and grimaced. "Good decision. I don't know how the early settlers could stomach this."

~

TRAFFIC across the bridge flowed briskly in both directions. As they reached the mainland they passed a crew in a power truck, likely headed for the island.

Cell service! April was delighted to see her phone bleep as it delivered a slew of messages, but before she could read any of them the low battery warning flashed. So much for getting back in touch with the world. She turned off her phone and put it away.

Baxter pulled into the first fast food drive-in they came to and ordered coffee and breakfast sandwiches for two. He didn't seem any more inclined than she did to make small talk before they reached the airport where he did his pre-flight check and filed his flight plan. The ground crew pulled the steps over.

It all seemed to take forever, but April felt reassured by Baxter's attention to detail before he finally took his seat, put on his headset and started communicating with unseen air traffic people. With luck, they'd be back in a matter of hours. She took the same seat she'd started out in last time and buckled in before she plugged her phone into the charging station next to her. She had just used the last of her phone's battery power to text Robert her arrival time.

From the cockpit, Baxter turned his head her way. "Should be a smooth flight home."

She hoped so.

~

ONCE HOME, it was like she'd never been away, never been stranded in a storm-ravaged cabin with Baxter. Conversations between them were strictly business, with him adjusting his post-production schedule where possible to accommodate events she had him scheduled for, like the upcoming high school visit.

A few photos with them in the background at the wedding cropped up on various social platforms, but no mention of either of them by name. It seemed there'd been many other, far more interesting guests in attendance.

She was pondering a way to get Baxter's full name out in the world before Vivica did, when inspiration struck. She had the high school film teacher introduce him by his first name. Then she posted a picture of him and the class with the caption, "Director Ernest Baxter Reid, looking earnest as he shares his knowledge with fledgling film students."

The students thought the play on words was hilarious, and the post went viral immediately.

Unfortunately, hers wasn't the only post featuring Baxter to go viral.

"I HOPE you're not disappointed we're not actually going to be on set, filming anything," he told the eager young grade twelve student whose name he had drawn from the students at the high school. "But a director's job involves a lot more than that one aspect. Our day today should give you a pretty accurate look at some of the behind-the-scenes work that goes into a production."

Sandy, he hoped that was her name since it was what he'd been calling her all morning and she hadn't corrected him, nodded seriously and pushed her glasses up her nose, only to have them slip back down to where they'd been resting.

His protege took photos of everything and appeared to write down every word he said as if it was gospel. He had to admit, he was surprised by the caliber of knowledge the girl displayed and the intelligent questions she asked. At her age, he hadn't a clue what he wanted to do with the rest of his life. Except not turn out like The Captain.

He ignored the funny look from his crew when he introduced Sandy and said she'd be shadowing him all day. "One of the things they don't emphasize enough in film school, at least they didn't when I was there, is how important a role the trust factor plays."

"You mean trusting yourself?" Sandy asked.

"No, the people you hire. Dave for example, my editor. We've worked on several projects together in the past and it took a while to build that trust, to accept that there are times when his vision might surpass mine in how the final cut gets edited together. Other times I feel like he's in my head, he knows me so well."

"Is that why it's been so hard for women to break into the industry? Because men don't trust them."

Baxter released a sigh. He'd been expecting a question along these lines. "It's more a matter of men and women seeing things differently. Women see things from an emotional place. Men focus on the physical reality."

"So, you'd think a combination of both ways of thinking and viewing things would be the perfect mix to strive for, providing that balance."

Baxter couldn't argue. He also wasn't about to tell her that wasn't often the way things were done. She'd find that out herself.

"After a number of years, once you've built up the trust

factor with someone, it's hard to start all over with someone new."

"Which is why the industry has always seemed a little closed against newcomers," Sandy said.

"Listen, it's always been hard for anyone new to break in. It takes a lot of dedication, a lot of hard work and a really thick skin. Someone that's too sensitive won't have what it takes."

She skewered him with a look. "And women are considered softer and more sensitive. Is that it?"

"I didn't say that."

"You implied it."

He faced her, arms crossed over his chest. "I'm aware that certain factions of society have been underrepresented in the entertainment industry, but everyone I know is dedicated to seeing that change."

She nodded. "It's about time the wrongdoers were called out."

"Listen Sandy, this is a work day, not a political rally. Now are you ready to move on?"

"Of course, Mr. Reid."

As they sat together and went through the editor's cut, he explained his strategy when they filmed certain segments and how Dave's vision had edited them together seamlessly. He showed her his well-thumbed script scribbled with notes and changes. He explained the way directors were frequently forced to pivot, anything from a sudden weather change affecting outdoor scenes, or a simple matter of an actor getting sick.

He was surprised when Sandy suddenly looked at her watch, rose and extended her right hand his way. "I understand you have another commitment at four o'clock, and this has been great, Mr. Reid. Thank you for taking the time with me today, I know you're busy."

"Not quite the glamor job a lot of people assume, is it? What happens next for you?"

"On the contrary, today was invaluable and I'll be sharing everything we talked about today with my class-mates. I hope you'll consider doing this again next year with a different group of students."

He was aware April had shown up a short time ago, trying to be unobtrusive. "You hear that, April? Apparently, what I had to say was invaluable."

April rolled her eyes as she moved to his side. "We try not to build up his ego too much, Sandy. But I'm glad you got some useful insights."

"Thank you for arranging for Mr. Reid to visit our class. Some of the others expected him to be an arrogant egotist. At least that was the general perception from what we've seen of him."

"As we know, perceptions are often false."

"Well, thank you both, again."

Baxter turned to her once they were alone. "Where were you when I was fending off barbs about discrimination and lectures about lack of opportunity for women and visible minorities in the industry?"

"I'm sure you handled yourself like a pro."

"It went okay. What else have you got up your pretty little sleeve to humanize the beast?"

"Well, I was thinking about putting you on the block for a bachelor auction. Good cause and all that."

"Isn't that objectifying men?"

"Depends who you talk to. But since you're supposed to be my boyfriend, you're off the hook because you're not available."

"Score one for the fake date." He gave an exaggerated sigh of relief. "If we weren't supposedly a couple, would you have at least shown up to bid on me in case no one else did? I mean, that would be the worst. A guy puts himself out there for a worthy cause only to get publicly humiliated when no one wants him."

"Baxter, it's not like you to display a streak of insecurity. What happened to that devil-may-care attitude of yours?"

"Someone hinted it was the wrong attitude to get me what I want."

It was also the mask he had perfected, the Baxter Reid he presented to the outside world. The one April had stripped away,

CHAPTER 11

"**G**reat news!" Mike's voice all but chirped over the phone.

"I could use some," Baxter said. Frankly, he was getting tired of running in the media wheel, seeing and being seen at all the screenings, cocktail parties, fundraisers, nominations parties and everything else April dragged him to.

"The studio is asking you in for a meet-and-greet."

"I haven't done one of those in years. Haven't I been elevated above the novice, entry-level posturing?"

"Not this time, buddy. Not when we are introducing them to the new and improved Baxter Reid."

"Why do I feel like I've been anointed with Holy Water and absolved of all my sins?"

"I like that image. Hang onto it. Along with your Boy Scout cap."

"Should I resurrect my sash with my Boy Scout badges?

"Have you still got it?"

He hoped Mike was kidding.

"Text me the time and place and I'll be there." He added the info to his phone, then stood and stretched. He almost called April to share the latest update, then stopped himself. He didn't want her to think he was looking for an excuse to call. Which, if he was honest, he was. Which seemed silly when the rest of the world thought they were a couple.

After their island getaway, she'd retreated back behind the safety of her car and driver. It bugged him that he didn't know where she lived; was never permitted to pick her up or drop her off after one of their many public appearances.

Still, if this studio summons was anything to go on, her image makeover campaign had worked. A meet-and greet-meant the studio was one step closer to choosing their director. Which meant his tour as April's boyfriend was also coming to a close.

For some reason, the thought didn't sit very well with him.

His phone chimed. April. Almost as if she knew she was foremost in his thoughts. Was it possible? Could there be something to the theory about a serendipitous connection between two individuals?

He scoffed at himself before he answered the phone. Look at him, getting in touch with his feminine side. "Hey, there! I was just thinking about you. Did you hear the news?"

"I did. Congratulations!"

"I think we both deserve credit. What do you say we get together and celebrate later?"

"I'm sorry, I can't tonight."

"Some other time, then." He hung up, unable to fathom his disappointment. What the heck was going on here?

APRIL STARED at her silent phone, disappointed in herself. She'd wanted so badly to say yes to Baxter's offer. Which was precisely why she'd said no. That, and there was a family thing tonight. A family thing she was dreading.

Her father was turning sixty-five. Which she didn't consider much of a milestone in this day and age when people were living so much longer than earlier generations, but the family was throwing a big bash. Even her mother was going, along with her second husband and lord knew who else. April had never wrapped her head around the fact that everyone other than her liked to pretend the Thomas-Rogers-Whiteheads were one big happy family. A happy family where she'd never truly belonged.

In typical frugal fashion the party was potluck, hosted by her dad's wife, Mel, in their home. She picked up some salads and crustini canapes she'd ordered from the deli, then took the food home and packed it into brand new plastic food savers, even though she doubted anyone would be fooled into thinking she made any of it herself. Mel's oldest daughter had this annoying habit of praising whatever April brought and asking for the recipe, which April sensed was a trap and sent her scouring Dr. Google to find a recipe that looked similar.

She'd put up with countless numbers of her stepsister's belittling antics when they were younger and her adult self refused to give Dakota the satisfaction.

Dakota must have been watching for her. "You're still using the driver service?" she asked before April even had her coat off or put the food on the table with the rest.

"That's right."

"I thought you would have moved on by now from what happened all those years ago. Are you still seeing that counsellor?"

April shook her head.

"I'm sure if you were, she'd say the same thing. Nothing good comes from carrying this kind of stuff around or letting it impact your behavior."

"It's a long drive," April said tightly. "I get a lot of work done on the way."

"I guess that's something. It's not like you're a big drinker and need a DD," Dakota said.

April was spared further barbs by the arrival of her mother with Sam, April's stepdad. Funny how similar Sam was compared to her dad. As if Lily hadn't learned anything from her first marriage.

Then again, maybe April was more her mother's daughter than she thought, since Lily hadn't appeared to move on so much as choose a replacement as close to the original as possible.

The door kept opening and closing as newcomers arrived and April managed to slip into the background the way she'd always done when she was younger. It was Liam who found her alone in the corner and slipped his tiny hand wordlessly into hers. She bent down.

"Lotta people, hey?"

He nodded, eyes wide with a wisdom beyond his years.

"You like your cousins?" For her part, she'd long given up trying to keep track of the offspring of various steps and half-siblings.

He shrugged.

"I get it buddy."

"Can we go to the park again one day?"

"Sure. I'll work it out with your mom."

He nodded again and ran off to play.

"Work what out with me?" Mackenzie took Liam's place

and passed April a glass full of liquid bubbles. "I spritzed it for you. Lots of soda, small splash of wine."

"Thanks." It felt good to have something to hang onto, and a drink in her hand gave the illusion she was one of the family.

"I half-expected you might show up with Baxter," Mackenzie said with studied casualness.

A thought which had also crossed her mind during their recent call for one insane second, before she banished it.

"I make it a point not to mix family and friends."

"You sure that's all he is? A friend?"

"I told you before not to believe anything bandied about by any of the social platforms."

"The wedding on the island looked fun."

"It was a very classy event," April said, "even though I wore my flip-flops."

"Did he fly you both up in his plane?"

"He did."

"That's something you wouldn't have done a short time ago. I guess being Baxter's 'friend' agrees with you," Mackenzie said before she wandered off. A short time later Mel called for everyone to grab a plate and 'chow down'. Her dad, who was heading the lineup at the table, beckoned her over and passed her an empty plate.

"Happy birthday, Dad." She leaned over and kissed a slightly grizzled cheek. "Does this mean you can get a government handout after all these years?"

"It's not a handout, Princess, it's an entitlement for all my hard years of servitude."

She followed her dad along the array of dishes lining the family's massive dining table, aware of veiled looks from some of the others who always felt she'd been favored over them. "Does this mean you're planning to slow down and take a trip or something extravagant?'

"Nah. But it does mean I'll have more time to work on my golf swing." He looked around. "The girls thought you might have a date in tow for a change."

"Fake news," she said, looking around, wondering what Baxter would make of the situation if he'd come with her. "Tell Mel not to read the gossip columns."

He shook his head. "Ever since Dakota turned her on to Petranella's People, she's addicted."

"Oh, life in La-La-Land," April said with a laugh, and went to find an empty seat.

APRIL HAD BEEN on pins and needles ever since Baxter's meet-and-greet with the studio came and went, and still no formal announcement as to who would direct *Sentry*. She'd done her best. From here on, the rest was up to him.

Which also meant she began to taper off the time they spent together. Earnest Ernest had a shiny new image he appeared to be living up to. Industry faithfuls reported that director Baxter Reid was broadening his hiring practices for his next project, giving some newbies a shot at working with him.

Hints and speculation that he was also a contender for *Sentry* continued to circulate, but nothing official. She knew the wheels ground slowly at the inception of a film project, and only much later would things careen out of control with impossible schedules and deadlines.

She'd never felt this invested in a project, and the realization was unsettling. Baxter was a client. The job was nearing an end. So why was letting go so hard?

She took her angst and unanswered question to her self-defense class.

"Whoa! Who are you mad at?" asked her instructor as she flipped him onto the mat. He sprang to his feet and faced her as April circled in full defense mode.

Herself! She was mad at herself for becoming emotionally involved. For not keeping her distance. Even her and Baxter fake-dating had been a dumb idea.

Except it worked!

At least as far as Project-Baxter was concerned.

Suddenly she was on her back, staring at the ceiling.

"You lost your concentration," her instructor chided, holding out a hand to help her up. "That's not like you."

It was worse than that. During Project-Baxter she'd let down her guard, released her control, even allowed someone else to make decisions for her. None of which were the way she operated.

She faced her instructor and bowed. It was time to move on.

So, when a grateful former client invited her to meet him for drinks, she accepted. She knew being seen publicly with an influential political figure would arouse speculation; exactly her intent. The first step in letting it be known she and Baxter had drifted apart. She let something similar slip to a few other influencers. Not a splashy break up. That wouldn't be beneficial to either of them.

"So tell me. Are we officially broken up or on a time out?" Baxter asked her next time she called him.

"Neither," she said.

"That's not what the gossips seem to think."

She made a disbelieving snort. "You never read that stuff."

"No, but Mike does religiously. And it seems awfully

suspicious that at the same time you start to fade out of my life, my enemies are suddenly hard at work stabbing me in the back."

"What do you mean?"

"Did you know I didn't get *Sentry*?"

April sat down abruptly. "When did you hear?"

"MCU is releasing a press release later today. At least they were nice enough to give me a heads-up so I didn't hear it through the rumor mill."

"I don't understand." When she realized her hand was cramping from gripping the phone too tightly, she set it down and switched it to speaker.

"We both knew it was never a sure thing."

Except she'd believed, from all accounts, Baxter had been the front runner.

"Sorry to smash your all wins, no losses record." He sounded bitter. "Baxter, what's really wrong?"

"Nothing. Other than the Image Queen took the mighty Lion King and turned him into a docile house pet, one who can't be trusted not to slip back into his old ways. Earnest Ernest is a fraud, or so 'they' say."

"Who is 'they'?"

"I guess you've been too busy with your new boyfriend to read what's being said about me lately, but the allegations started out fairly subtle, shortly before you were seen out and about with someone else. Since then, things have escalated. A lot of backstabbing smears from someone who knows me, or at least knows more than they should about me. Someone who knows things about my family. About my background. Out there in such a way that it rings true."

Oh no! He thought she was responsible! "Baxter, where are you? I'm coming over."

There was a beat. Then another. "You want to hash this out face-to-face? You tell me where I can find you."

April hesitated a second too long.

"Thought so," Baxter said. "Your distrust of men since you were carjacked is legendary. Which is another reason everything about this smear campaign points to you."

April blurted out her address, not bothering to ask how he knew about her being carjacked. "Come over right now. We'll get to the bottom of this together."

April's home smack dab in the middle of single-family suburbia with a park down the block was not even close to what he'd expected.

He'd been disappointed over the news about *Sentry*, but the loss was nothing compared to the loss and betrayal boiling his blood at the thought April had turned on him. First she'd rejected him, then she'd muddied his name.

He'd calmed by the time he reached her door. Jumping to conclusions was the old Baxter MO, and never solved anything. It was in his best interests to hear her out, to convince her to stop.

He knocked on her front door, looking around at the neat and tiny, unpretentious yard, the fading blooms and dying greenery of the garden beds signaling another cycle finished. Much like what he and April had been to each other. One cycle in the wheel of life.

She opened the door cautiously, as if not sure what to expect on the other side, or what kind of mood he might be in.

"Nice place," he said when she ushered him in.

"It serves my needs. Would you like some coffee?"

He shook his head. "Did you check out social after we spoke?"

"I did and I have to admit it appears someone has it out for you. Someone with an axe to grind who's been biding their time, waiting for an opportunity when you have something to lose."

"Mike said the same. He's seen this kind of thing before. At first, he thought it might have been the competition, but he got hold of the shortlist for *Sentry*. None of this smacks of their handiwork. Now that I've calmed down enough to realize it's not you—"

"I'm happy to hear you say that."

He nodded. "Knee-jerk reaction to you giving me the public brush-off." He noticed she didn't try to refute his words. "My money's on Vivica or one of her cohorts at Blaze's wedding."

"I had a different thought," April said. "I have a half-sister named Mackenzie. Does that name mean anything to you?"

"Should it?"

"Apparently you dated her once. Although what she considered a date, I'm not sure. She downplayed her involvement with you when she thought you and I were an item, but she also warned me I'd need to hone my self-defense skills."

Baxter tensed. "I have never raised a hand to anyone, male or female. Not after growing up around my old man."

"I know that. In hindsight, I think she might have meant in the emotional sense rather than the physical. Especially if she, herself, had formed an emotional attachment to you years earlier."

"I don't even remember her, sorry."

"She has a three-year-old son. She's never told anyone who the boy's father is."

Baxter reeled. "And you think—"

"I don't know. She was so offhand about you and I, I wondered if it was a case of 'she who doth protest too much'."

"Not that you asked, but I have always been very careful to make sure none of my old man's bloodline gets passed down to future generations."

They were interrupted by a frantic-sounding summons at the door. April's face grew pale as her eyes flew to meet Baxter's. Immediately his protective instincts were aroused.

"I'm not expecting anyone. And only a handful of people know where I live."

"Don't answer, then. It's probably just someone trying to sell you something."

"Maybe." But as she checked the security camera on her phone the banging on the door continued, followed by a female voice calling April's name. "It's my sister."

The second she opened the door, a young woman burst inside. "What took so long?" Then she looked past April to where he stood near the back of the room. "Why is he here?"

He eyed the newcomer, a faint memory stirring in the back of the gray matter. April's sister. She'd been a stand-in on one of his movies years ago. Always acting like she was bound for better things and was doing the cast a favor by being there. That the job was beneath her.

She'd tried to seduce him once, hung around after everyone else left. Said she knew that's the way most acting careers got started and she was willing to pay the price. He'd sent her packing, pink-slipped her and forgot about her.

Mackenzie folded her lithe frame into a chair. After

exchanging looks with him, April perched on the couch. He remained standing.

"Whatever the two of you might think, it wasn't me."

If anything, April went even paler. "What makes you believe such a thought crossed our minds?"

"There were some quotes from long ago. Things Baxter said to me that I didn't take kindly at the time, but that I probably deserved."

Baxter blew out a breath. How was he supposed to remember every wannabe that came onto set or what he might have said years ago? But apparently this woman, this Mackenzie, hadn't forgotten. He decided to play along.

"That's right, Mackenzie. Things I said, easily taken out of context."

"I was dumb," Mackenzie said. "And naïve. I took exception to what you said, and—and I might have vented to another person. Someone I thought I could trust. I'm sorry, April. I didn't realize how much she despises you. That she'd drag up all this to sabotage your business and make it look like it came from me."

"Who?" April appeared to be as much in the dark as he was.

"Dakota."

The name shed no light for him, but apparently meant something to April.

APRIL HAD no idea how Mackenzie managed it, but Dakota did an immediate cease and desist on dragging Baxter's name through the mud. Luckily, people in Hollywood had short memories and things quickly returned to some semblance of normal. Not that anything felt normal now

with Baxter totally out of her life. She found herself remem-
bering the smallest details about him. The way he held the
wheel, whether he was driving a car or piloting his plane.
Strong capable hands, almost one with the powerful vehicle
under his control. His kindness when he made her tea
during the storm. He probably even let her win at Cribbage.
And there had been his genuine empathy toward the children at the hospital. The way he really took what she said to
heart and tried to be a better person.

In the end, she trusted him implicitly, something she'd
not been able to say about any man since that scary night
years earlier. More than that, she missed him. Even his stubborn streak.

"April," Mike said over the phone a few weeks later, "I
need one more thing from you."

"You have another difficult client for me?"

"Same difficult client," Mike said. "You need to work
your magic and convince that stubborn SOB to take the
Sentry job."

"I thought the show went to someone else."

"Originally. But the arrogant jerk-wad negotiated
himself out of the deal."

"So they approached Baxter."

"Through me. He refuses to discuss it. Said he wasn't
their first choice, it's their loss, blah, blah, blah." Mike
sighed. "I know it's what he wants, deep down, but he can't
handle the idea that he was rejected."

April started. He'd been the same toward her, acted out,
feeling rejected when she gave him the gentle media
letdown.

"Mike, if he won't listen to you, he certainly won't listen
to me."

"April, I've known Baxter for a long time. You're the only

one who's ever gotten through to him. You're good for him. He was a different guy when you two were together."

"We weren't actually together."

"It might have been an act on your part. But Baxter treated it like the real thing. I might add, he's been a bear lately to everyone who crosses his path. If something doesn't change, he's going to torpedo his career for real."

April hung up and stared out the window. If Baxter set a course to self-destruct, there was nothing she could do to prevent it. Or was there?

BAXTER STOOD STARING at the headstone. The veteran's cemetery, usually a drab, colorless place with matching headstones resembled a poppy field today, thanks to the hundreds of artificial red poppies that adorned every grave. The old man had died of emphysema after a lifelong love affair with cigarettes, which had been enough to make Baxter swear off tobacco products at a young age. Living with second hand smoke probably hadn't helped his brother's asthma when they were young. He ought to look Browning up one of these days and see how he was doing. Maybe they'd go together to visit their mother. Maybe it would be easier with both of them. Maybe he was tired of doing everything alone.

Clinging to his old beliefs wasn't exactly doing him any favors. Maybe the smart ones *were* the guys he knew who'd taken the plunge, got married and started a family. What was the saying about married men living longer than their single counterparts? Only for the chance to be a thorn in the side of their partner, or so he used to think.

He heard someone behind him, someone else come to

pay their respects, no doubt. He saluted the headstone, turned around and banged into April, who stood looking at him with those wide, expressive eyes.

He waved a hand to encompass the cemetery. "You have someone here as well?"

She shook her head.

"I don't understand."

"I hoped I might find you here, seeing as it's Veteran's Day." Her voice sent a shiver of sensation down his backbone as she slipped her hand into his. "Burial parks can be lonely places for the ones who are left behind. I thought you could maybe use some company."

He felt an inner wariness seep through him. What was her agenda now?

As soon as the thought surfaced, he squashed it. That was the way the old Baxter would think. He linked his fingers through hers and glanced down at their joined hands. They looked right. Felt right. Like they belonged together.

He pulled her close. "That was really thoughtful of you. I could use the company."

She raised a slightly trembling hand to his face, smoothed his cheek with her palm. Then she raised up on her tiptoes and kissed him.

He gathered her against him as he kissed her back, felt her sigh of release matching one from him as they sealed a promise for a shiny new future.

"I've been wanting to do that for a long time," he admitted later, when he could finally find his breath, his arms still around her tight, her head against his chest, one hand nestled in the back pocket of his jeans. "But I knew about your past, and I didn't want to— I don't know, make you even more leary of me. So I kept my distance."

"I felt the same, but I was so afraid of making myself vulnerable; keeping firm control of every situation was how I coped."

"I had things to let go of, too." He waved toward Ernest Senior's grave. "Fear of turning out like him. I have a bad habit of rejecting others before they get a chance to reject me."

"I didn't reject you, Baxter. I was confused."

"That makes two of us."

'What's this nonsense I hear about you turning down *Sentry*? It's everything you want."

"You're wrong about that. You're everything I want, and accepting the show means I'd be out of town for at least eight months. I couldn't stomach the thought of being away in case you ever needed me."

"I do need you, Baxter. I also need you to direct the film of your heart. You'll do a better job than anyone else could."

"You're probably right about that. Any chance you'd consider coming with me if I accept the show?"

"No consideration needed. I'm all in." She sighed and nestled against him. "Before the attack, I always wanted to travel. Afterwards, I was too afraid. What if it had been my fault, and I unwittingly provoked someone else?"

"That's as unfounded as me being afraid I'll turn out like my old man, may he rest in peace. You and I have a life to build. Together."

"I agree. Starting now."

Baxter kept his arm securely around her as they started toward the parking lot. The guys were going to have a field day when they learned about this. He might have been the last man standing, but now he was more than ready to foray into a new phase of his life with April. A life the two of them built together. He tightened his arm around her. A life together. He like the sound of that.

Thank you for picking up a copy of *Baxter (Last Man Standing)*.

If you enjoyed reading it, please tell others by leaving a review wherever you purchased *Baxter* or on Goodreads or BookBub.

If you haven't already done so, check out the other wonderful books in the Last Man Standing series.

The story starts with Baxter making a toast at Blaze's stag. If you'd like to find out how Blaze met Kaitlin, keep reading for an excerpt from *One Fantasy Fall*.

~

"You're early." Kaitlin opened the door to see a man clad in dusty, formfitting leather, his shaggy caramel-colored hair badly in need of a trim. She stepped back a pace. "Come on in. Let's see what you look like under all that road dust."

The stranger stepped past her and into the front hall. "You must be Kaitlin. Steve said—"

"One good thing. We should be able to fit you off the rack." Kaitlin circled the man, eyes narrowed as she inspected him. In the right clothes, this one should clean up quite nicely. Broad shoulders tapered to lean hips, which were hugged by a modern-day version of cowboy chaps in supple-looking black leather.

"But those chaps. All wrong unless you're auditioning for a cowboy commercial." The garment in question sheathed him like an intimate glove, up over snakeskin boots to hug an impossibly long length of leg, before ending in a V of faded denim below his belt. The scrap of exposed denim was the exact same shade as his eyes. Realizing where her gaze lingered, she looked away and hoped she wasn't blushing.

He rocked back on his heels and crossed his arms over his impressive chest. One side of his mouth quirked up in an endearing half-smile. "I wasn't expecting an audition."

Dead silence hung between them and Kaitlin felt herself flush. Weren't people supposed to outgrow adolescent blushing? Apparently not her. Even her ears were burning.

"Somehow, I get the feeling you're not my brother's friend/wannabe model I was expecting."

"Is that what he told you?" The newcomer braced one shoulder against the doorframe as if he had every right to be there, thumbs hooked in the pockets of his jacket.

She blew out a breath that didn't do a thing to help cool her down. "I'm sorry. Were you looking for Steve? He's at work right now."

His half-smile turned into the real thing. The change in expression deepened the grooves in his cheeks and gave him a lazy look that matched his careless pose.

His smile was addictive and Kaitlin caught herself starting to smile back.

"How about I introduce myself properly? The name's Blaze." Lazily his right hand stretched toward her, broad and sun-browned with a faint line of scars visible across the first two knuckles. "I'm your date for the weekend."

Order *One Fantasy Fall* today.

If you enjoyed visiting *Baxter*, you might also enjoy:
Blue Sky Island
One Cinderella Spring
One Stolen Summer
One Fantasy Fall
These books don't need to be read in any particular order.

Spring 2023 I'm part of a new contemporary series, *Always a Bridesmaid.*

Hint: You met Frannie at the beach wedding. Watch for her story.

Better yet, sign up to my VIP Readers Newsletter to receive a bonus novella, the latest freebies, sales and updates. http://eepurl.com/bVosbI

You might have guessed I write mainly about cowboys, Wild West and Contemporary Times, with the occasional playboy thrown in for good measure.

See more on my website KathleenLawless.com

ALSO BY KATHLEEN LAWLESS

Western Historical Romance

Grace's Folly

Anora's Pride

Callie's Honor

Maddy's Fugitive

Widows, Babies and Brides - Box Set of the 4 Books

Sweet Western Historical Romance

SEVEN BRIDES FOR SEVEN BROTHERS SERIES

Brody's Bride - Book 1

Bradley's Bride - Book 2

Braydon's Bride - Book 3

Blake's Bride - Book 4

Bishop's Bride - Book 5

Barron's Bride - Book 6

Benjamin's Bride - Book 7

Seven Brides for Seven Brothers Box Set 1 - Prequel & Books 1 to 3

Seven Brides for Seven Brothers Box Set 2 - Books 4 to 7

Sweet Western Historical Romance

WIDOWS OF THE WILD WEST

Hope

Janie

Sweet Western Historical Romance

MAIL ORDER BRIDES

Mail Order Olivia

Mail Order Rachel

Mail Order Martina

A Bride for Shane

A Bride for Riley

A Bride for Weston

Mail Order Noelle

Chelsea's Choice

Here Come the Brides - Volume 1

Here Come the Brides - Volume 2

Sweet Contemporary Romance

Baxter

Blue Sky Island

One Cinderella Spring

One Stolen Summer

One Fantasy Fall

One Wondrous Winter

Sweet Christmas Romance Novellas

Holly's Wish

No Groom at the Inn

Steamy Historical Romance

Taboo

Unmasked

Steamy Contemporary Romance

SECRET SEDUCTIONS

Her Untamed Cowboy - Book 1

Her Undercover Cowboy - Book 2

Her Unwilling Cowboy - Book 3

Who Needs a Cowboy! - Book 4

Intimate Strangers

Women's Fiction

Fabulous at Fifty

Romantic Suspense

Final Heat

Afterburn

For a complete book list visit KathleenLawless.com

To be the first to hear about Kathleen's new releases, special fan pricing sales, and also receive a free book, sign up for her VIP Reader Newsletter at http://eepurl.com/bVosb1

ABOUT THE AUTHOR

USA Today Bestselling Author, Kathleen Lawless, blames a misspent youth watching Rawhide, Maverick and Bonanza for her fascination with cowboys, which doesn't stop her from creating a wide variety of interests and occupations for her many alpha male heroes.

With nearly 50 published novels to her credit, she enjoys pushing the boundaries of traditional romance into historical romance, contemporary romance, romantic suspense and women's fiction.

She makes her home in the Pacific Northwest and loves to hear from her readers.

~

Sign up for Kathleen's VIP Reader Newsletter to receive updates, special giveaways and fan-priced offers. http://eepurl.com/bVosb1

KathleenLawless.com
Goodreads | BookBub
Facebook | Instagram | TikTok

ABOUT THE AUTHOR

USA Today Bestselling Author, Kathleen Lawless, blames a misspent youth watching Rawhide, Maverick and Bonanza for her fascination with cowboys, which doesn't stop her from creating a wide variety of interests and occupations for her many alpha male heroes.

With nearly 50 published novels to her credit, she enjoys pushing the boundaries of traditional romance into historical romance, contemporary romance, romantic suspense and women's fiction.

She makes her home in the Pacific Northwest and loves to hear from her readers.

Sign up for Kathleen's VIP Reader Newsletter to receive updates, special giveaways and fan-priced offers. http://eepurl.com/bVosb1

KathleenLawless.com
Goodreads | BookBub
Facebook | Instagram | TikTok

goodreads.com/kathleenlawless

bookbub.com/authors/kathleen-lawless

facebook.com/kathleenlawlessnovels

instagram.com/kathleenflawless

tiktok.com/@kathleenflawless

www.ingramcontent.com/pod-product-compliance
Lightning Source LLC
Chambersburg PA
CBHW022022170626
46808CB00003B/1028